Balance

Omega Queen Series, Volume 9

W.J. May

Published by Wanita May, 2021.

This is a work of fiction. Similarities to real people, places, or events are entirely coincidental.

BALANCE

First edition. May 20, 2021.

Copyright © 2021 W.J. May.

Written by W.J. May.

Also by W.J. May

Bit-Lit Series
Lost Vampire
Cost of Blood
Price of Death

Blood Red Series
Courage Runs Red
The Night Watch
Marked by Courage
Forever Night
The Other Side of Fear
Blood Red Box Set Books #1-5

Daughters of Darkness: Victoria's Journey
Victoria
Huntress
Coveted (A Vampire & Paranormal Romance)
Twisted
Daughter of Darkness - Victoria - Box Set

Great Temptation Series
The Devil's Footsteps
Heaven's Command
Mortals Surrender

Hidden Secrets Saga
Seventh Mark - Part 1
Seventh Mark - Part 2
Marked By Destiny
Compelled
Fate's Intervention
Chosen Three
The Hidden Secrets Saga: The Complete Series

Kerrigan Chronicles
Stopping Time
A Passage of Time
Ticking Clock
Secrets in Time
Time in the City
Ultimate Future

Mending Magic Series
Lost Souls
Illusion of Power
Challenging the Dark

Castle of Power
Limits of Magic
Protectors of Light

Omega Queen Series
Discipline
Bravery
Courage
Conquer
Strength
Validation
Approval
Blessing
Balance
Omega Queen - Box Set Books #1-3

Paranormal Huntress Series
Never Look Back
Coven Master
Alpha's Permission
Blood Bonding
Oracle of Nightmares
Shadows in the Night
Paranormal Huntress BOX SET

Prophecy Series
Only the Beginning
White Winter

Secrets of Destiny

Revamped Series
Hidden
Banished
Converted

Royal Factions
The Price For Peace
The Cost for Surviving
The Punishment For Deception
Faking Perfection
The Most Cherished
The Strength to Endure

The Chronicles of Kerrigan
Rae of Hope
Dark Nebula
House of Cards
Royal Tea
Under Fire
End in Sight
Hidden Darkness
Twisted Together
Mark of Fate
Strength & Power
Last One Standing
Rae of Light

The Chronicles of Kerrigan Box Set Books # 1 - 6

The Chronicles of Kerrigan: Gabriel
Living in the Past
Present For Today
Staring at the Future

The Chronicles of Kerrigan Prequel
Christmas Before the Magic
Question the Darkness
Into the Darkness
Fight the Darkness
Alone in the Darkness
Lost in Darkness
The Chronicles of Kerrigan Prequel Series Books #1-3

The Chronicles of Kerrigan Sequel
A Matter of Time
Time Piece
Second Chance
Glitch in Time
Our Time
Precious Time

The Hidden Secrets Saga
Seventh Mark (part 1 & 2)

The Kerrigan Kids
School of Potential
Myths & Magic
Kith & Kin
Playing With Power
Line of Ancestry
Descent of Hope
Illusion of Shadows
Frozen by the Future
Guilt Of My Past
Demise of Magic
The Kerrigan Kids Box Set Books #1-3

The Queen's Alpha Series
Eternal
Everlasting
Unceasing
Evermore
Forever
Boundless
Prophecy
Protected
Foretelling
Revelation
Betrayal
Resolved
The Queen's Alpha Box Set

The Senseless Series
Radium Halos - Part 1
Radium Halos - Part 2
Nonsense
Perception
The Senseless - Box Set Books #1-4

Standalone
Shadow of Doubt (Part 1 & 2)
Five Shades of Fantasy
Zwarte Nevel
Shadow of Doubt - Part 1
Shadow of Doubt - Part 2
Four and a Half Shades of Fantasy
Dream Fighter
What Creeps in the Night
Forest of the Forbidden
Arcane Forest: A Fantasy Anthology
The First Fantasy Box Set

Watch for more at www.wjmaybooks.com.

Copyright 2021 by W.J. May

THIS E-BOOK OR PRINT is licensed for your personal enjoyment only. This e-book/paperback may not be re-sold or given away to other people. If you would like to share this book with another person, please purchase an additional copy for each recipient. If you're reading this book and did not purchase it, or it was not purchased for your use only, then please return to Smashwords.com and purchase your own copy. Thank you for respecting the hard work of the author.

All rights reserved. No part of this publication may be reproduced, stored in or introduced into a retrieval system, or transmitted, in any form, or by any means (electronic, mechanical, photocopying, recording, or otherwise) without the prior written permission of both the copyright owner and the above publisher of this book.

This is a work of fiction. Names, characters, places, brands, media, and incidents are either the product of the author's imagination or are used fictitiously. Any resemblance to actual person, living or dead, events, or locales is entirely coincidental. The author acknowledges the trademarked status and trademark owners of various products referenced in this work of fiction, which have been used without permission. The publication/use of these trademarks is not authorized, associated with, or sponsored by the trademark owners.

All rights reserved.
Copyright 2021 by W.J. May
Balance, Book 9 of the Omega Queen Series
Cover design by: Book Cover by Design

No part of this book may be used or reproduced in any manner whatsoever without written permission, except in the case of brief quotations embodied in articles and reviews.

BALANCE

Have You Read the C.o.K Series?

The Chronicles of Kerrigan
Book I - *Rae of Hope* is FREE!

BOOK TRAILER:
http://www.youtube.com/watch?v=gILAwXxx8MU

How hard do you have to shake the family tree to find the truth about the past?

Fifteen year-old Rae Kerrigan never really knew her family's history. Her mother and father died when she was young and it is only when she accepts a scholarship to the prestigious Guilder Boarding School in England that a mysterious family secret is revealed.

Will the sins of the father be the sins of the daughter?

As Rae struggles with new friends, a new school and a star-struck forbidden love, she must also face the ultimate challenge: receive a tattoo on her sixteenth birthday with specific powers that may bind her to an unspeakable darkness. It's up to Rae to undo the dark evil in her family's past and have a ray of hope for her future.

Find W.J. May

Website:
https://www.wjmaybooks.com
Facebook:
https://www.facebook.com/pages/Author-WJ-May-FAN-PAGE/141170442608149
Newsletter:
SIGN UP FOR W.J. May's Newsletter to find out about new releases, updates, cover reveals and even freebies!
http://eepurl.com/97aYf

Balance Blurb:

USA Today Bestselling author, W.J. May, continues the highly anticipated best-selling YA/NA series about love, betrayal, magic and fantasy.

Be prepared to fight... it's the only option.

Who says you can't go home again?

When a crimson dragon rises from the ancient fortress, Evie and her friends think their luck is finally turning. Their enemy is strong, but not invincible. He is raising an army of darkness, but they have powerful allies to come to their aid. They are returning to their parents. Their parents will know what to do.

If only things were so simple.

A realm divided cannot stand, and it will require more than taking up the crown again to restore the five kingdoms. Sacrifices must be made, an impossible choice that shakes the friends to their very core.

Are they willing to do what is required? Can they set aside personal happiness for the greater good?

No matter what they're forced to give...will it ever be enough?

BE CAREFUL WHO YOU trust. Even the devil was once an angel.

The Queen's Alpha Series

Eternal
Everlasting
Unceasing
Evermore
Forever
Boundless
Prophecy
Protected
Foretelling
Revelation
Betrayal
Resolved

The Omega Queen Series

Discipline
Bravery
Courage
Conquer
Strength
Validation
Approval
Blessing
Balance
Grievance
Enchanted
Gratified

Chapter 1

There comes a point in every dream when the consciousness begins to stir.

Walls shimmer and boundaries fade. The laws that govern grow weak and confusing. Two worlds battle for dominance, each rattling the confines of the other, and for a moment—just a moment—one finds oneself stranded on the edge in between.

Whether the dreams be a blessing or nightmare, that fleeting moment is always accompanied by the faintest trace of fear. An instinctual resistance to the transition. The loss of one world, to be replaced by the next. The fear is universal, forgotten by the time one awakens.

This is SO much worse than that.

Evie flexed the tips of her wings, careful not to disturb the silent group of people gathered in the dip between her shoulders. They shifted anyway, peering restlessly over the sides.

For the last three days, they'd been flying in a straight line east.

Rather, the dragon had been flying. The friends had been clinging to the crimson scales, closing their eyes and trying desperately to convince themselves that they weren't hurtling through a cloudless sky. The journey had been largely uneventful. They rested when she needed. They flew when she was ready. Aside from an unfortunate hunting incident, wherein the princess had rather enthusiastically used her new powers to 'help', things had been quiet and unchanging in the skies.

Until now.

Three days they'd been flying. And the journey was said to take three days. Of course, none of the friends could vouch for this. None of them had ever travelled so far outside the kingdom. But according to Cosette, the only one to have visited before, things were starting to look familiar.

Adelaide had wept for joy upon hearing the news.

The others...had not.

What will they say? Evie thought, not for the first time. *What will they say when they see us?*

In her mind, it was a joyful reunion. Lost child comes back from the dead. There would be rejoicing, laughter, stories, wine. All those tender hands she'd so dearly missed would rise up to embrace her. She would be wanted. She would be home.

But her heart knew better.

This was our choice.

In spite of the chaos that had risen up around them, it was impossible to dispute this one damning fact. While they had no way of predicting what madness would ensue—the years of prolonged travel, the sorcerer's dark curse—the friends had chosen to leave. More than that, they had made use of a terrible opportunity just to steal that first breath of freedom.

Whatever bitter memories had followed—the grieving, the conflict, the dissolution of all unity in the realm—it would be fair to say they had chosen that as well.

Not fair, perhaps. But depressingly accurate.

What will they say?

In no world could Evie imagine her mother not crying at the sight of her. Despite her fearsome reputation the Damaris queen had always been free with her emotions, caring not who happened to witness such a spectacle. Yes, her mother would weep at the reunion.

But would they be tears of joy? Or had the window for such sentiment passed? Was it all part of the same tainted memory, their entire journey, lost in the wretched abandonment of the past?

And what of her father?

A blurry image flashed through her mind, coming back on the wings of a dream. The broken king kneeling on the bank of a rushing river. His head bowed in sorrow, his face streaked with tears.

"Are you all right?"

The quiet voice of the vampire whispered over the air, gentle as a breeze and as easily dismissed by the others. With the bond between them, he rarely had to ask. But he asked anyway.

Does he not know? Does he not feel this way himself?

It would be impossible to know whether such emotions were shared as strongly during the transformation. But judging by the way his hands tightened on the base of her neck, offering a faint squeeze of reassurance, she'd be willing to bet he understood it quite well.

She stretched her wings again, forgetting her promises to keep steady.

No, she thought, though he was unable to hear, *I'm not all right*.

The only comfort, and it was indeed a small one, was that she wasn't alone. That feeling of dread had overtaken them all. She could feel the tension rolling off the others, disguised in tight smiles and glances at the passing scenery, though their fingers were clutched white upon her back.

When she alighted suddenly on the crest of a mountain, she felt their relief as well.

"Okay..." Freya said uncertainly, releasing her death grip. "I guess we're stopping?"

The process went a lot smoother than expected, considering the friends had little experience with such things. The second her feet touched the grass the others jumped to safety, while Ellanden lingered a step behind to offer a helping arm to her grandmother. Once they were clear, the princess began the uncertain task of 'removing the dragon' whilst the others waited at a safe distance. This part was always a bit trepidatious, but no sooner did she feel the chilled alpine wind bite into her skin than Asher was there with his cloak, draping it over her with a gentle smile.

"Welcome back." Those dark eyes scanned her carefully, always seeing more than they should. "How are you feeling? That was the longest time yet."

Shifting was a delicate balance, especially to those just starting out. In what felt like another lifetime, Evie remembered her father cautioning the new wolves in the infantry. Warning them not to push themselves too far, lest those lines blur a little too deeply and the beast begin to take hold.

It was always said as a joke. It was always said over ale. But standing atop the mountain, shivering in the vampire's cloak, she couldn't help but worry there was some truth in it.

"It's becoming too much," she admitted, pulling the fabric closer around her. "I'm glad that we're almost—"

But she caught herself suddenly, unable to lie.

"I know," Asher said softly, his hands closing over hers.

Their eyes met briefly, sharing a silent understanding, then flew in opposite directions as the rest of their friends trudged forth. Although the dragon was technically the only one at work, the others would later swear it took just as much a physical toll to ride along as passengers.

The fae, in particular, was having problems.

"That was unbearable, as always." He shook out his cloak and made a spectacularly failed effort to smooth back his hair. "I will never understand, Everly—given that you are the *only* thing up there—why it's somehow impossible to fly in a straight line. Have you been drinking on the sly?"

"Quit it," Cosette chided, looking him over with a grin. Seeing as the princess of the Fae was gifted with dragon blood herself, she didn't mind the screaming winds nearly so much as her intemperate cousin. "You aren't fooling anyone. The adrenaline junkie doesn't like to fly? The only reason you're complaining is that you're jealous you can't manage such a thing yourself. Or out of some belated sense of loyalty to your father—who has grown *past* his misgivings, by the way."

Half-true.

Given the mutinous flash of the fae's eyes, the jealousy was most definitely real. But his father was no closer to taming his hatred of flying than the first moment one of his best friends transformed before his very eyes. The last time he'd been forced to take to the skies, the highborn prince had actually feigned a convenient poisoning rather than climb upon the dragon's back.

That being said, the mention of his father had made a profound impression on the young prince. His eyes flew without thinking towards the distant mountains before retreating quickly to the safety of his shoes. He murmured without thinking in his native language before catching the others watching and switching quickly into the common tongue.

"That's ridiculous. Only a fool would amend themselves to such things."

...that's not what you said.

"I'd much rather fly alongside of my *own* volition—"

"Then grow wings like your mother and take to the skies," Asher said dismissively, turning back to his girlfriend. "Sweetheart...why did we stop?"

Lies failed her. Excuses failed her. Those mountains were looming up behind him, just as inescapable and distressing as they'd been to the fae.

"I had to sneeze," she blurted, adding a quick, "Don't want to do *that* as a dragon."

It was a testament to the absurdity that Ellanden agreed with it immediately. The rest continued staring, as if waiting for something more. It took a moment to realize what that was.

"...it passed."

In the quiet seconds that followed, the princess wished *very much* that she'd come up with something better to say. Her friends graciously averted their eyes while her grandmother stepped forward, easing her hands away from the vampire to take them in her own.

"My sweet girl...there is *nothing* your parents want more than to see you home again. You must not trouble yourself, there is nothing to fear—"

"I'm not afraid," Evie shot back evenly.

A few paces away Ellanden stiffened arrogantly, as if rebutting the words himself.

The queen's eyes twinkled and she pulled in a patient breath. After years of presiding over the Damaris court, she was well-used to navigating such delicate egos. But by now even the vampire was staring at apprehensively at the mountains, a trace of panic flickering in those dark eyes.

"You think they will be angry," she said softly, glancing back at the others before returning her gaze to the trembling girl. "You think this is something they cannot forgive. Better they live with a memory. Better they think it was never your fault."

Such a simple summary of a writhing mess of feelings.

Evie glanced away quickly, forbidden tears stinging the corners of her eyes. She had half a mind to leap straight off the cliff, returning only when she was armed with fangs and scales, but her grandmother squeezed her fingers tightly—forcing her to return that steady gaze.

"But it *wasn't* your fault, dear one. You set off to save the world, only to fall victim to a dark enchantment. Do you really think that *your parents* won't understand such a thing?"

The princess pulled in a sharp breath, wanting so badly to believe that was true.

"But we left," she whispered, unable to meet the woman's eyes. "We slipped away in the aftermath of a grisly attack, knowing full well—"

"That was ten years ago."

Adelaide said each word softly, but they cut to the core. Whether it was a reassurance or further condemnation, the princess wasn't sure. But one way or another, it settled the question.

"Take it from someone who knows…"

Those twinkling eyes grew abruptly sad.

"It is their every prayer, their every thought, their every aching dream." She cupped a hand around the princess' cheek. "The very breath in their lungs…it is all longing for you."

THE DRAGON TOOK TO the skies just moments later, soaring in the blaze of a radiant sunset as the last of their endless journey slipped quickly away. After only a few minutes, Cosette abandoned her perch beside Seth and slid to the base of her cousin's neck, giving it a quick squeeze.

"It's just there," she pointed to a cluster of peaks in the distance, "can you see?"

Evie nodded faintly, making a wide turn.

She saw where the little princess was pointing, but didn't quite understand what she was looking at. The mountains may have been under enchantment, but they looked no different to the outside world. The base was a valley, the slopes were a forest…but the peak?

The peak had been replaced with a sprawling villa that would have looked at home in any one of their kingdoms. No possible clue how it got there. It simply materialized out of thin air.

You can take the queen out of the castle…

Not once, not twice, but three times the dragon circled—ignoring the increasingly pointed stares from its passengers, pretending to debate where to land. It wasn't until she heard Seth's quiet voice, "I'm going to be sick," that she decided to take the plunge.

Not a moment too soon, since there was about to be another dragon in the skies.

They heard the argument before they saw it, angry voices drifting up on the breeze. A second later, they glided into view and saw the pacing figures of two people.

People as familiar as the friends themselves.

Serafina...Kailas.

"—past time I went to look for her!" the Damaris prince was shouting. "I don't care if she'll resent the intrusion, I can't believe it's taken me this long!"

The enchanting fae trailed behind him, fire burning in her eyes.

"I'm not disagreeing with you! I'm simply coming along!"

Each time her husband took a compulsive step towards the stone ledge that ran along the villa, she grabbed him back again. Each time she did, he wrenched himself out of her grasp.

"I don't care what might be out there, Kailas! You're not looking for her alone!"

The handsome prince whirled around to face her, his eyes so dark from lack of sleep the shadows at the bottom seemed to overtake his entire expression.

"You may not care what's out there," he hissed, "but I've *seen* it! You cannot ask me to risk losing you—you are my *wife*!"

"And she's my daughter," Serafina shot back evenly. "I was not asking for your permission, Kailas. But you're more than welcome to give me a ride."

The shifter tensed ever so slightly, staring over the edge.

"Those are your parents?" he asked softly.

Cosette blushed and bit her lip.

"They're usually a bit more even-tempered than that."

That might have been true once, but that time had clearly passed.

Tasked with protecting the one surviving child, the young couple arguing on the terrace wasn't the same as the one that Evie and the others had left behind. The couple that smiled easily and laughed at the wilder tempers of their friends. The crowns of abandoned kingdoms had fallen upon them. The crushing mantle of a broken family had been theirs to uphold.

They had done the best they could, balancing between two worlds.

Torn between their own grief and the need to hold things together. Between councils and kingdoms. Between allowing their daughter to live her own life and their own crippling terror that those cruel fates would return to claim the precious girl they'd missed.

It was an impossible task, and the years had taken their toll. But it was equally impossible to miss the tender affection still burning in their eyes.

"I would never ask you to stay behind," Serafina said more quietly, oblivious to the giant shadow creeping towards them in the sky. "You cannot ask such a thing of me."

Kailas laughed shortly, but wrapped his hands around hers.

"No...you would sneak out before sunrise. Leave me tied to the bed."

She gazed up at him with those clear, sparkling eyes.

"Darling, you have *never* minded me tying you up before."

Another quiet burst of laughter, though the words were less well-received up above.

Seth and Freya glanced at Cosette with the same wicked smile, while the fae princess looked like she was going to be sick. The only one who matched her expression was the stately woman sitting beside her—the one who'd just glimpsed the new adult version of her son for the first time.

Let's take another lap, shall we?

"Don't even think about it," Asher murmured, guessing her thoughts. "If you don't land soon, they'll take off themselves. We don't want to meet under those circumstances."

...fair point.

The first time Evie had seen her uncle fighting with a sword, she'd had nightmares. Such a thing was immeasurably worse when the man fought with the powers of a dragon.

After taking a deep breath she circled back around, dipping low enough now to get a better look at the people speaking down below. Her uncle was still angled towards the edge of the terrace, though he continued to hold his wife's hand. And Serafina's hair was not flowing in loose waves like the princess had always remembered, but was gathered in a tight knot on the back of her head.

She lifted her eyes as the dragon flew towards them, and for a split second that exquisite face shadowed with a hint of fear. Fear was replaced with confusion. Then shock. Then finally—

"By the stars..."

Even so high above them, the princess heard it clearly—the ancient saying spoken by the fair folk since time itself began. It spurred her faster as she streaked towards the balcony, lowering her nose in a controlled dive only to pull up suddenly and alight upon the cool stone.

A moment later, she felt that stone beneath her bare feet. A cloak was draped quickly over her.

Then all was quiet and still.

Say something...say anything...

It seemed the most impossible task of all. There was not a whisper of sound between the two groups, not even a breath. The friends were frozen in a huddle, the breathtaking fae was rooted to the spot, and Evie was starting to think she'd have handled it all better as a dragon.

Only Kailas found a way to break the spell, taking a faltering step forward as his mouth fell open in absolute shock. Those dark eyes travelled from person to person, widening with each one.

On his daughter returned safely home.

On the children he loved as dearly as his own.

On the woman standing beside them, her eyes shining with tears.

At that point a strange look came over him, fluttering his eyelids, and he stepped back again, believing himself to have wandered into some kind of dream.

"...Mother?"

Adelaide crossed the distance between them, one hand clasped over her heart.

"My darling boy." She reached the tips of her fingers to his face, lingering there a moment before gesturing to the people behind her with a watery smile. "We have come home."

Chapter 2

*H*ome. The word seemed to resonate between them, and yet it didn't quite fit. This place, despite their parents' recent attachment, was no one's home. The friends had never been there before. The only one to have visited had only done so a handful of times. It was a strange villa, built awkwardly atop the world's loneliest mountain, and yet...it was filled with the people they loved.

So it is a home, then...in a way.

The others cared less for semantics, although they were so overwhelmed they could hardly be counted on to speak. Kailas and Adelaide were the only ones yet to have managed, and once they'd done so it seemed to have taken all their strength with it. They stood now merely gazing at each other, lost in a kind of daze. One, searching her memory. The other, remembering a portrait.

"You..." Serafina had never been the speechless type, but after seeing that her daughter was alive and well she found herself staring at the others with something close to wonder. "How is such a thing possible? You're...alive. You're here."

Neither was phrased as a question, yet there was a question in them all the same. One the friends found themselves suddenly incapable of answering. Cosette glanced their way then took a step towards her parents, those dark eyes resting a moment on each face.

"They've been trapped...by a wizard. Trapped in an enchanted sleep. When they awoke, they believed it had only been a few weeks. But the sorcerer held them for years."

Her mother and father stared back—*stunned*. She blushed and lowered her eyes.

"...you knew I was looking."

Kailas stared a moment longer then lifted his gaze to the others, shaking his head. "Still..." he murmured incredulously. "After all this time..."

There was much to be said, much more than the friends even realized. But although their long journey had finally ended they found themselves breathing quickly, suddenly pressed for time.

Ellanden took a bracing step towards his aunt then paused just as quickly, his bright eyes sweeping away from the terrace and towards the rest of the dwelling.

"Where is my father?"

The lovely woman couldn't speak but her eyes shot behind them towards a secluded balcony, as if the fae in question spent so much time there his presence could be assured.

The prince took off without another word, moving at a speed that was hard to follow. His friends followed nonetheless, and almost ran into him when he froze suddenly atop the steps.

His father was standing on a smaller terrace below him, staring into that endless horizon.

There was a moment when everything paused. When the friends froze and Ellanden sucked in a quick breath, staring at the back his father's head—those familiar ivory braids same as his own.

"Cada."

His voice echoed softly, calling for his father in the language of the Fae.

Cassiel tensed, but didn't turn. If anything he seemed to sigh, his eyes blurring as one sunset melted into another. "Trouble me not here," he murmured. "For I am miles away."

Evie threw a quick glance at Asher, but he was just as bewildered as she.

Ellanden went still for a moment then took a halting step forward, trembling from head to toe. When he could go no further, he tried again—raising his voice a little louder.

"*Cada.*"

Cassiel's head tilted towards them, then he turned. A wave of shock passed between them, almost a tangible thing, then his face went perfectly still. For a few seconds that's how he remained, nothing more than a statue. A lovely, tragic statue to complete the melancholic beauty of the garden.

Ellanden took a step closer, trying to force his face into a smile but having just as hard a time with it. When he passed an invisible line Cassiel actually stepped back, but was stopped by the balcony wall. His son froze abruptly, a hand stretched uncertainly between them.

"Is this a dream?" Cassiel breathed. "I've had so many dreams..."

His voice trailed into a whisper, and some part of Ellanden came back to life. His brow tightened with a fleeting pain before he crossed the remaining distance between them, laying both hands firmly upon his father's arms. They were but inches away, staring right at one another.

"It's not a dream," he said softly, squeezing at the same time. "It's me. I'm here."

The famed warrior glanced down with a shiver, staring at the long fingers wrapped around his arms. It was the first time the princess had failed to see him meet a moment. It was the first time she realized it was possible for her invincible uncle to bleed.

Time itself suspended, giving the pair an endless moment, then Cassiel blinked quickly and leaned back—eyes sweeping over every inch of his son. From the tips of his boots to the top of his head. One hand lifted hesitantly to Ellanden's shirt while the other came up to the ivory hair, longer than his father had ever seen, still twisted with the braids he'd helped teach him as a child.

He lingered there a moment, then moved quite suddenly—cupping the back of his head.

"Ellanden."

It was an affirmation. A resurrection. A broken promise come to life.

Tears slipped down the prince's face as he nodded, biting his lip and leaning into the hand, unable to believe he'd ever convinced himself it was all right to walk away.

For as long as they were still, they embraced just as suddenly.

Cassiel gripped him with such strength that the prince's face tightened with a grimace of pain. He never said a word. Not even when his father's arms tightened still further, lifting him straight off the ground. It was a heart-wrenching scene, and one that could very well have gone on forever if Cassiel's eyes hadn't flown open with a sudden thought.

"Tanya!" he called in an urgent, rasping voice.

All eyes shot expectantly to the doorway, waiting for the woman to appear. But the others found they could wait no longer. Like a cheetah scenting the breeze Asher lifted his head suddenly, his dark eyes leaving the terrace altogether and fastening on a particular place within the villa.

Aidan.

He was off like an arrow, flying across the stone, straight past the tiny Kreo queen who was just happening upon the garden, the one who'd stopped as though struck by lightning, staring at the fae. Evie hurried after him as he raced through the gardens, realizing with a sudden horrible pang that the lovely halls had been designed to look just like the house in Taviel—the one where the families had gathered every year since she'd been born, filling it with all their happiest memories.

He literally ran into his father as Aidan was coming up the stairs. Both men grabbed hold of each other for balance before freezing abruptly in place.

"...Ash?"

Never before had the princess seen such an expression. It was as though something had pierced straight through her uncle's chest, leaving him suspended in the grip of a blade. The younger vampire couldn't speak—he merely nodded, hands tightening around fists of his father's sleeves.

Their people did poorly with abrupt transition, unless they were the catalyst of such things themselves. Neither did they have any patience for illusions or tricks. Most things were done with blinding speed, but others moved at their own pace and could never be rushed.

This particular truth dawned slowly, like a sun rising hesitantly above the trees.

Aidan's eyes swept over every inch just as slowly as Cassiel had done, seeing past the time and distance to a thousand fractured memories, lost in between. He took half a step closer, slipping a hand into his son's dark hair. The other lifted to his own mouth, pale and trembling.

"You're here."

It was said with no certainty. As if he'd walked into a thousand empty rooms, travelled to a thousand desolate places, and declared the same thing before. His fingers tightened and his eyes shone in the fading, dusky light. Then slowly, he leaned forward—inhaling that lost, familiar scent.

It was the scent that convinced him. Vampires had always been primal about such things.

"Asher."

His arms came together like a vise—closing around his son with a pressure that threatened to kill him. To heads came together, a blending of raven hair. He was murmuring beneath his breath, too fast and low for Evie to hear, but she was no longer trying.

Her blood was on fire as her feet flew over the stone.

Looking back on it later, she'd never understand how she knew which way to go. The villa was sprawling, and while it was designed in a similar fashion to the house at Taviel the things and people occupying the rooms were not the same.

Down one corridor she flew, then up another. It had gotten to the point where her head was spinning and she found herself gasping for breath. Then all at once, she came to a sudden stop.

The door was cracked open, just scarcely ajar, but she could still see the beautiful woman on the other side—perched on a stool in front of a vanity, eyes fixed blankly upon the mirror.

There was a sound behind her as more people flooded into the hall. Another woman was rushing towards them, but the princess never noticed. With trembling fingers, she pushed the door.

"...Momma?"

When was the last time she'd used such a phrase? Not since she was a child had the word escaped her lips. But Katerina turned as if no time had passed, spinning gracefully on the chair to face her daughter just as she always had...then freezing with the same blank stare.

"...oh."

Her lovely face stilled without a shred of expression, a stark contrast to her daughter who was still trying to catch her breath. When Adelaide appeared suddenly as well, trembling like a leaf, the queen leaned back against the vanity with a horribly pragmatic, "I'm dead."

...what?

She didn't sound upset, merely surprised. As the two women froze in the doorway her gaze drifted to the window, almost as if she expected to see that mystical enchantment finally fail.

"I wonder what happened..."

Evie's head jerked and she took a faltering step inside.

She wanted to contest it. She wanted to shake her mother loose, to scream at the top of her lungs until the suffocating stillness that gripped the beautiful villa shattered once and for all.

But she stood in helpless silence as Katerina pushed to her feet with a smile.

"You found her." She swept across the room in four graceful strides, squeezing her mother's hand before turning to her daughter. Their eyes came together for a suspended moment, then she smoothed down both sides of the princess' hair with a warm smile. "You found her before I did."

Evie's stomach knotted as her head shook back and forth.

This isn't right. None of this is right.

"You're not...you're not dead." She gestured quickly between them. "*We're* not dead. I came back. Grandmother Adelaide...we met in the woods. She helped me to find you."

An impossibly unlikely series of events. One that defied even the most capricious of the fates. One that required immediate explanation. Yet no explanation was required.

Katerina laughed quietly, tears spilling without notice down her cheeks.

"Of course you wouldn't accept it," she murmured. "You're too stubborn—your father's daughter, through and through." Her head lifted suddenly. "My husband...is he...?"

The door burst open and a breathless man appeared in the frame.

She rotated slowly to face him, remembering how he looked that first night she saw him, leaning against the filthy counter of a local tavern with the arrogance of a young god. Her eyes softened as she remembered the first time they fought together, kissed one another.

The day she married him in the glow of a blinding sun.

"Oh, sweetheart..." She said it almost like a sigh then held out a hand for him, turning back to her daughter with a heartbreaking smile. "It's what we wanted, Dylan. She came home. Now we can be together again...a family."

...a dead family.

"But I'm not—"

Evie's breath caught in her throat as she turned to her father for the first time.

The man suffered no delusions of death, neither could he spare his beloved wife more than a passing glance before he turned those sparkling eyes to his daughter.

There you are.

He took a single step closer, then rushed forward all at once—touching the tips of his fingers to her cheeks. She leaned into them without thinking, eyes blurring with tears.

"Father, I—"

He caught her a second later, holding so tight that she no longer had breath to speak.

A kind of exhaustion swept over her, settling into her very bones. Her eyes fluttered and she collapsed without thinking into those arms—arms that had never failed to catch her.

But a piece of her father had suddenly come back to him.

He offered a silent prayer, taking his first true breath in ten years.

"*...thank you...*"

Such changeable hands—light as a ranger, strong as a king—swept through her hair, tangling by intention, anything to keep close. Their foreheads touched and his breath caught with a quiet sob.

"Where have you been?"

She pulled back just far enough to see him, just far enough to see her mother standing a few steps behind. Just far enough to see an alpine sunset glowing in the open window.

I could ask you the same question.

Chapter 3

The friends spent the night in their parents' chambers. Though it was never even bashfully admitted, most of them slept in the same bed. They hadn't been given a choice, though they might have crept inside anyway. Their parents were physically incapable of letting them go.

They were also physically incapable of sleep.

While the children succumbed to the fatigue of the journey, resting peacefully for what felt like the first time in ten years, their parents watched tirelessly in the darkness. Never blinking, never moving, glancing up only occasionally to stare into each other's eyes.

Not until later would Evie realize they'd never even considered going to sleep. Close their eyes in slumber…then awaken to realize it was all a dream?

Not in a thousand restless years.

By the time the princess blinked open her eyes, rays of sunlight were already pouring in from the eastern window. They danced in little patterns across the bedspread, dazzling her eyes as her mind awakened slowly, trying to remember where she was.

Over the last few months, she'd laid down her head in so many different places it would be a miracle if she could keep them all straight. Everywhere from a tundra to a tavern. From a cave, to a swamp, to the light of a hundred campfires—each blending into the next.

Very few of them had come with a blanket. Even fewer had come with a roof.

The birdcage had been particularly memorable.

"…turned out to be an old terium mine…"

She rolled over and looked across the room to see two women standing by the window. In profile, they could have passed as twins. The same tall, slender stature. The same tumbles of fiery red hair. They even sounded the same, the soft murmur of voices blending in her ears.

She hitched up onto an elbow, then dropped back down—hunkering under the covers as the pair continued speaking quietly amongst themselves.

Since streaking down from the sky on a pair of scaly wings she'd most definitely *not* had before, it had been a toss-up as to which existential revelation would take priority. The resurrection of dead children. The resurrection of a dead mother. The unmentioned abandonment of the royal crown. And none of this was even to mention the discovery of a Damaris prince born of a wizard.

Admittedly there were some pressing matters to discuss, but the princess could only hope her grandmother was catching the rest of them up, because she wanted no part of it. All she wanted was to lie in that magnificent bed and close her eyes until the rest of the world faded away.

"Honey?"

Or not.

She peeled the blanket back slowly, bracing for the worst. But whatever heavier storylines the women had been discussing had been hidden behind a pair of identical pearly-white smiles.

"Would you like some breakfast?" Katerina perched on the edge of the mattress, stroking back her daughter's hair. "You must be starving. I know exactly how much energy it takes to…"

…to fly?

The silent implication hung between them, catching each off guard. For a split second those smiles faltered, time stalled, and the princess' fingers edged towards the blanket once more.

She swung her feet to the floor instead. "Breakfast sounds great."

AS IT TURNED OUT, THE princess wasn't the only one to seek refuge in the dining room. By the time she rounded the corner, bare feet padding across the stone, the fae were already at the table.

"Morning," she murmured, slipping into a chair against the wall.

Ellanden looked up with a tight smile, but Cassiel was in his own world.

There were two plates in front of them, but only one had been touched. The other hadn't even been filled. Their chairs had been dragged unabashedly together and her uncle still had an arm around his son's shoulders...the same way it had remained for the duration of the night.

Ellanden had learned to navigate around it.

Under most circumstances such a gesture would have been met with instant teasing, but the young fae would never dream of pulling free. Quite the contrary, he seemed oddly protective of his father; glancing over every few minutes with a sweet and unprompted smile.

"Morning," he echoed, keeping his tone deliberately light. "How did you—"

"More toast?"

Evie glanced up with a start as a steaming platter appeared in the doorway.

Tanya had clutched her son, she'd counted his breaths, she'd clocked his heartbeats. She'd spent the night secretly crying into his hair. Now, she seemed determined to feed him to death.

Ellanden held up a hand, but there was no point in refusing—it was already sliding onto his plate. The princess' eyes widened at the sheer quantity before drifting to the kitchen.

Where do they keep it all?

"...thank you." Ellanden lifted an obliging forkful to his mouth before lowering it just as quickly, looking vaguely sick. "You know, we've been well-fed at the fort—"

"Yes, darling."

Tanya brushed him off quickly, refilling his glass for a third time. A kiss to his forehead then she was back in the kitchen, pausing only to give Evie's hand a bone-shattering squeeze.

...I should have stayed in bed.

There was movement in the adjoining hallway, a soft echo of feet. The two friends glanced up hopefully, feeling a bit like captives in their chairs, but no sooner had Seth appeared in the doorway than he froze uncertainly—wishing he could slip right back out.

If it wasn't so breathtakingly awkward, the princess might have laughed. For all his jokes back at the fort about his introduction to royalty, he certainly didn't look eager for it now. Quite the contrary, he cast a single glance into the kitchen and every muscle in his body locked down. One foot was actually hovering an inch off the floor, as if he'd stepped onto cracked glass.

"I'm sorry..." He trailed off nervously, eyes sweeping the silent table. "I didn't...I didn't think anyone else would be awake yet."

Are we that early?

The princess glanced out the window, while he retreated back into the hall.

"You must have a lot to talk about—"

"Nonsense," she interrupted quickly, desperate for a buffer. "Pull up a chair."

Those dark eyes flickered past her, to the pair of immortals perched motionlessly on the other side of the table. He stared a moment without blinking, then shook his head a little too fast.

"No, it's fine. I was actually going to—"

"Seriously, Seth—take a seat." Ellanden glanced pointedly at the table before lifting his eyes in supplication. "Nothing better than a family breakfast."

The shifter flashed a tight smile. "Then you should enjoy it—"

The princess and the fae spoke in unison.

"*Please.*"

The young man threw them both a swift look of betrayal, but wouldn't dare refuse. Instead he forced a gracious nod, silently calculating how long he might be required to stay.

It was a testament to his level of unease that he sat down next to Ellanden—glancing once at Cassiel's imprisoning arm before deliberately ignoring it, just as the prince was doing himself.

He took a plate when it was offered, blanching at the molten pieces of toast. "This looks...wonderful."

Ellanden glanced over with the hint of a genuine smile, tipping some of his own onto the shifter's plate. "Save me from a cardiac event," he muttered, then louder, "It's best when eaten hot."

So you can't taste it. So it burns straight through your mouth.

Caravast was a traditional Fae delicacy. But after Tanya Oberon's 'modifications', it bore little resemblance to the original thing. The others had adjusted by simply scalding their palates into nothingness.

The shifter was not so lucky.

He leaned over cautiously as swirls of steam wafted into his face, then glanced to the side in confusion as Ellanden tossed him a roll of utensils and continued with his own plate.

"...with a fork?" he asked in surprise. The fae nodded. "But it's bread."

A generous assessment.

It was 'bread' in the same way that wine once claimed to have grown in the sun. Somewhere in between, there was a putrification process. Hence, the copious amounts of syrup.

The shifter's dark eyes narrowed suspiciously.

"Are you serious?"

"I swear," Ellanden vowed, cutting off a piece for himself as proof. "Try it."

With that same distrustful look, Seth lifted a bite to his mouth—only to stiffen with an involuntary grimace. He did his best to hide it, summoning all the manners his mother had drilled into him as a child. But the best of intentions could only stretch so far.

"It's...uh..."

There was a crack in the tension and princess snorted into her drink.

A chorus of laughter swept over the table, loosening those coiled muscles as the friends clutched the edges of their chairs. Just a fleeting moment, but it came not a moment too soon.

"That's terrible!" Seth took a swig of water, forgetting for a moment to be afraid. "*Terribly* sweet. How could anyone eat such a thing?"

The laughter vanished and a chilling silence sprang up in its wake.

"Oh, let me guess." Seth glanced from one person to the next, a smile still lingering on his face. "It's some mystical Fae-thing, right? An ancient recipe called down by the heavenly ancestors?"

There was a little pause.

"No," Ellanden replied softly, looking down at his plate, "...my mother made it."

At that precise moment, Tanya breezed in with a smile. "How's the toast?"

The boys glanced at each other.

"*Great.*"

"*Great.*"

She deposited another mountain of it on the table then swept straight back the way she'd come, leaving a strained silence in her wake. Evie and Ellanden cheerfully ignored it, turning back to their breakfast with a genuine grin, but Seth shifted uneasily, glancing two chairs down.

"I'm sorry," he stammered awkwardly to Cassiel. "I meant no offense. I don't...I don't even know what to call you. My lord?"

The words felt strange and unfamiliar on his tongue. Not since he was six years old had such titles been relevant. Since then, his little village, too small to earn a nick on the map, had drifted so far from those royal tethers it had never been heard from again.

That being said, he'd guessed correctly.

The fae shied away from words like king. It was enough of a stretch to call Ellanden a prince and Cosette a princess. Their sovereign was simply referred to as the Lord of the Fae.

When the shifter's question went unanswered, Ellanden gave his father a little nudge.

"Cada...?" he prompted gently. "He asked what to call you."

Cassiel glanced up suddenly, as if awakened from a trance.

Since the trio had sat down at the table he had been little more than a statue beside them, giving not the slightest reaction to anything said. The only time he'd even registered their presence was to close his eyes ever so briefly at the sound of his son's laugh.

"You can call me whatever you like," he replied softly. "You saved my son's life. More times than I'll ever know..." He trailed off, then caught himself. "You can call me whatever you like."

A blush stole into Ellanden's cheeks as he stared at his plate. The others stared for only a moment before averting their gaze as well. A second later, they were eating in silence once again.

You saved my son's life...

The princess pushed the toast around her plate, chewing on her lower lip.

So her uncle had gotten more of the story, at least enough of it to be unsurprised there was a teenage shifter eating at his table. Seth had undoubtedly saved Ellanden's life many times over. They had all saved each other. After so many weeks, then months, technically *years*, fighting side by side, such a thing had become common enough to escape memory.

But how much did Landi tell him? Does he actually know the—

"Good morning."

She lifted her head as Aidan and Asher appeared in the doorway, ghosting into the room like twin shadows. Neither one looked at all rested, but there was a tired contentment in those dark eyes.

Because they spent the whole night talking, like any normal people would do.

A flush of guilt darkened her cheeks as she thought back to her own experience.

Having spent the previous three days flying across the realm as a dragon, a late-night recounting of the last ten years simply wasn't in the cards. She had stayed awake long enough to collapse into the arms of her father, long enough to press her face into the hands of her mother.

Then she'd demanded an offering of fruit and blacked out.

"Good morning," she said quickly, realizing Aidan was still waiting for a reply. She flashed him a welcoming smile before her eyes drifted to the handsome teenager standing by his side.

It was the first night she and Asher had spent apart since that fateful evening in the bell tower, after which no subsequent night had been the same. Another stunning revelation in a sea of so many others, but a single look at her boyfriend's face said he'd kept that particular one to himself.

Good. Very good. No need to share everything at once. We'll just act normal.

Their eyes met for a fleeting moment.

"Hi."

"Hi."

...like that.

Ellanden glanced up from his plate, staring between them with a truly wicked expression. But before he could say anything, a door swung open and Dylan breezed inside from the terrace.

He offered all the appropriate greetings, pausing behind Asher's chair to give his hair a quick ruffle, then circling gracefully around the table to sit at his daughter's side.

"Good morning."

His eyes twinkled as he reached into the pocket of his cloak, pulling out a pair of fresh mountain apples—the same kind they used to split when she was a child.

"You requested some fruit?"

She took one with a shy smile, scooting their chairs closer together.

The sun was drifting slowly higher as the rest of the villa came to life.

Doors were opening, voices were echoing, and more people were drifting into the dining room. Gathering together for a family breakfast, just as they'd done a thousand times in the past. At a glance, the scene couldn't have felt more familiar. All the same faces, the same smiles, the same seating arrangement at the table. Only upon closer inspection could one start to see tiny cracks.

It took Evie a moment to put her finger on it.

None of them is armed.

It was frowned upon for guests to carry weapons in Taviel, but you'd be hard-pressed to find a fae that wasn't at least armed with a blade. The High Kingdom had no such qualms, and in Belaria it was openly welcomed—a conversational piece that quickly escalated amongst the young wolves.

Given the people in question, it was downright bizarre. The princess couldn't remember a time when they hadn't been carrying enough weaponry to massacre a small town. The morning meal usually consisted of several casual demonstrations, which tended to crescendo as they neared lunch.

Yet here they were...not a blade in sight.

"—cial tae melios de larnessa—"

Serafina had bypassed the rest of the gathering altogether and was locked in a one-sided conversation with her nephew. He kept twisting around to answer, but couldn't escape his father's arm. In the end, she simply moved Cassiel aside and sat across from him—chattering at such speed that even the vampires, who had nearly as complete a grasp on the language, were unable to follow.

Evie was still watching when the door opened yet again.

Whatever conversation the Damaris queens had been having earlier, it seemed to have settled for now. They gave each other a quick smile before going their separate ways. Adelaide circled nearer to her son whilst Katerina paused suddenly, staring over the familiar scene.

"Looks like a full table," she murmured, unnoticed in the clamor.

Dylan pushed his chair back slowly, those bright eyes trained on her face. In no world could his beautiful wife ever go truly unnoticed, not while he was anywhere within sight. But before he could stand up and join her, she sucked in a quick breath and ducked into the kitchen with Tanya.

There was a pause in the clatter of dishware. It was followed by a muffled sob.

"It's fine," Dylan breathed, more to himself than his daughter. "Eat your apple."

Evie stared at the table, feeling slightly sick.

At the same time, her grandmother was looking slightly lost—pausing in the entryway without any idea where to sit. Kailas stood up quickly to offer his own chair—giving her a sweet, if slightly awkward, kiss on the cheek in the process.

"—haldarth maen culpanna—"

"—does anyone want more toast—"

Adelaide glanced around the table, resting her gaze on everyone she hadn't seen the day before. Just a cursory sweep to be reflected upon later, but her eyes paused upon the fae.

"I remember you..." She stared at Cassiel in astonishment, lost in another time. "You came to the castle with the rest of the High Born, cautioning against impetuous tempers, trying to guide my husband towards peace." There was a pause. "I'm afraid he wasn't very amenable to the idea."

Cassiel merely smiled, as if such things were long in the past. His eyes never left Ellanden.

Seriously...should have stayed in bed.

Dylan glanced between the queen and the fae before returning sharply to the latter. He studied him a moment, then leaned behind the table and pressed an apple into his hand.

"Eat something."

"I'm fine."

"*Now*, Cass."

To the princess' extreme surprise the fae lifted the apple to his mouth, taking an obliging bite before returning it to the table. Her father's eyes followed every move.

The door swung open a final time as Cosette and Freya stumbled in—wearing matching nightgowns and looking as though they'd gotten very little sleep.

But while the fae swept gracefully towards the kitchen, muttering under her breath about insomniac roommates, the witch froze abruptly in the doorframe just as Seth had done himself.

Between the two of them, she'd been genuinely delighted about the prospect of meeting fairytale royalty. But glancing around the table, it looked like she was rethinking that a bit.

Her eyes flashed between Evie—who was being force-fed apples, to Ellanden—who was officially a hostage, to Asher—who was seated so close to his own father she suddenly wondered if vampires ever drank each other's blood.

"...this is festive."

Seth lifted his head robotically, white-knuckle-gripping his fork.

"Sleep well?" he asked in a strained voice. "You should take a seat."

His eyes said something different.

Run!

The witch flashed an uncharacteristically sweet smile, vanishing back up the hall in a *poof* of smoke, but the shifter had drawn attention to himself at precisely the wrong moment.

"I don't think we've been introduced." Kailas slowly leaned forward, looking rather dangerous despite the casual smile. "My daughter checks in routinely, and I trust her to tell me anything of consequence, but I knew only of Freya...she never mentioned you."

Seth paled as white as the tablecloth, but was fortunately spared a response.

"He's a new addition," Cosette answered smoothly, emerging from the kitchen with a steaming cup in her hands. She took a seat beside her grandmother, never breaking Kailas' gaze.

It was a quiet standoff that could have lasted a small eternity, if Ellanden hadn't taken that very moment to remember he'd pledged support.

"Seth was a cage-fighter in Tarnaq," he said conversationally. "We actually met a ways before that, when he robbed us in payment to this gang, but...I guess it turned out well in the end."

In hindsight, he'd never been great at 'support'.

"He's a world-class shifter," Evie chimed in quickly, aiming a kick at the prince beneath the table, but accidentally getting Cosette instead. "And a *fantastic* guide. Isn't that right, Ellanden?"

"...fantastic guide."

"Cage-fighting in Tarnaq," Dylan repeated, looking the boy up and down. "I'm surprised you made it out in one piece. Must have put on one hell of a show."

Seth bowed his head with a blush, but Evie looked up suddenly.

"You know about Tarnaq?" she blurted. "You know about the arena?"

...and you allowed it to stand?

Ellanden shot her a quick look of warning, but he was thinking the same thing. They hadn't stayed long, but the place had left them with an abundance of memories from which to choose.

Perhaps it was the Carpathian lounging outside the café. Or perhaps the band of loathsome creatures who'd attempted to break into their chamber in the dead of night. Or perhaps it was the rampant slave trade that had left one of their closest friends fighting for his life.

Dylan opened his mouth to answer, then turned his face away. "Eat your apple."

Chapter 4

The princess stormed onto the terrace, feeling a little wild.

They had come to the mountain hideaway on a wave of adrenaline, propelled with the kind of momentum that left very little time to think. The body of a hellhound was burning behind them, the forces of darkness were rallying, and they had no earthly idea what the future had in store.

She'd assumed the reunion would be a blur, a tearful whirlwind of kisses and explanations, after which they'd set off once again upon their journey—two more dragons flying by their side.

There were stakes involved. These were weighted decisions.

It wasn't the time for stilted conversations over toast.

She truly didn't know which disturbed her more: Tanya's manic cooking, Serafina's incessant talking, or Cassiel's remote silence and the way her father kept pressing her with food. Her own mother couldn't remain in the same room without bursting into tears, Kailas had been thrust into a bizarrely uncharacteristic spotlight, and while Aidan was careful to keep a smile fixed on his face, every time his eyes strayed to his teenage son it looked as though someone had set him on fire.

We can't get caught up in this. We need to leave.

A cold truth settled upon her.

...they already did.

She and her friends had swooped in on the wings of a dragon, not to find a story in progress but one already finished. Their parents had ten years of adrenaline. Ten years of momentum. Each one leading to a greater heartbreak than the last.

They were dining with ghosts in the aftermath, refilling glasses and rattling chairs.

"Eat your apple," she growled under her breath, picking up a stray pebble and hurling it at the stone railing with all her might. It struck at a bad angle and flew straight back, slicing the top of her lip. For a second she merely stood there stunned, then she startled at the sound of applause.

"Who says royalty doesn't have a sense of humor?" Seth quipped, wandering out the same door she'd just escaped herself. "That was hilarious."

She tried to scowl whilst simultaneously catching the drip of blood before it could stain the top of her dress. Not a lot of clothing options when you were stuck on top of a mountain. Both she and Freya were both wearing things borrowed from Cosette.

"I live to entertain."

"Thanks for that," he said politely, joining her at the bannister and glancing casually over the side. "But if you're thinking of jumping, wait your turn. That's why *I* came out here."

"And why's that?" she said darkly, giving up on the lip. "You didn't enjoy family breakfast?"

Perhaps it was the blood still running down her chin, perhaps it was merely her tone, but Seth dropped the teasing and regarded her with a thoughtful stare.

"That was tough in there."

Her eyes flew ever so briefly to his face before settling somewhere in the middle distance. A place where she didn't have to see his expression, where she could revel in the misery all by herself.

"I didn't notice."

He smiled faintly, turning his back to the mountains and leaning against the rail. "And I can hardly see the blood all over your face."

She glanced at him again, then gestured angrily over the side. "Don't let me stop you—"

"What did you expect?" he interrupted quietly, staring into her eyes. "You've been imagining this moment since the day I met you. How did you expect it was going to be?"

She came to a sudden pause, thrown by that signature candor.

I expected them to have the answers. I expected them to have the drive. I expected them to fix things.

I didn't expect they'd be so broken themselves.

He stared at her a moment longer, almost appraising, then dug his hands into the pockets of his cloak. "I expected to be angry," he confessed.

Her eyes lifted tentatively, retreating the second he met her gaze.

"...angry?" she prompted.

He nodded, turning around again to stare over the slopes.

"This might have been your life, princess. But you were asleep in that cave for ten years. I grew up reading about your family, listening to tales told by the light of a hundred fires. The stories were true enough, but they read like lore...like fairytales."

His face warmed with the ghost of a smile.

"We were enchanted by them. These real-life heroes. Taking down evil sorcerers and monsters. Driving back armies of demons. A band of valiant warriors, fighting side by side."

There was a pause.

"...and then they left."

The princess glanced over quickly, startled by the sudden shift in tone. She couldn't hear it, exactly. His voice stayed low and even. But she could feel it. Something significant had changed.

"No one ever did more for this place than the people sitting at that table," he continued quietly. "And when you three went missing, they threw themselves into it all over again. Driving back the darkness, rooting out the corruption, holding things together with their bare hands. They didn't owe us anything further. Even from a young age, I could understand that. They had already united the realm, sacrificed everything they had to keep it together. When they decided to go, they left capable people in charge. Good, capable people...but none of that mattered."

He shook his head, staring at the distant trees.

"They left, and I hated them for it. My sisters grew up hungry. I was sold as a slave. None of those things were their fault. But they were perhaps the only people who might have stopped it, so I hated them all the same. They were *invincible*. The heroes from my stories. Where had they gone?"

Evie was looking straight at him, the rest of the world had melted away. "But you're not angry now?"

His eyes drifted back to the villa. "I was standing right here when your father raced onto the terrace. He'd seen the dragon and heard our voices, but he hadn't found you yet. The look on his face..."

He went very still, remembering. Then he shook his head.

"No one is invincible," he concluded softly, clapping her on the shoulder as he headed back inside. "And I could never hate that man. That man has been through enough."

<hr />

EVIE STAYED ON THE terrace a while longer, arms tight around her chest as she stared out at the birds. There weren't very many so high in the mountains; most had retreated to lower altitudes in search of warmth and food. The few that remained, she didn't recognize. Massive, predatory creatures, with a breathtaking wingspan and etched patterns on the feathers. They glided on the wind like silent sentries, those piercing eyes gazing into the forests below.

They were invincible. The heroes from my stories. Where had they gone?

A gentle breeze rippled the jasmine blossoms on the trees above her.

Here, apparently...

For almost half a decade the young monarchs might have torn the realm apart, searching for that which had been taken from them. But for the other half, they'd been living right there. A little villa on a lonely mountain, in a part of the world all but forgotten by the rest.

It was almost impossible to imagine.

How could they tolerate such confinement? Their restless parents, whose wanderlust had prematurely aged their councils and put uncharted territories on the map. How could they stand the isolation? Suspended in this lovely prison, gazing at the same horizon, day after day, year after year, while the rest of the world continued turning on the other side.

The sound of quiet voices drifted onto the terrace and she wandered away from the balcony, peering through the twisting jasmine into the garden below.

To anyone else, the sight would have been shocking. But the princess didn't think twice about the fae and the vampires sitting side by side. Curved stone benches had been placed in the shade beneath the trees in the garden. Ellanden and his father were on one, Asher and his father were on the other. A small table rested between them, gathering a steady layer of petals and dust.

"—hadn't decided anything for sure until that very moment," Ellanden was saying, his eyes locked upon the ground. "We fought the raiders alongside the rest of them. It wasn't until the attack was over and everyone was starting to regroup that…"

He trailed into silence, unwilling to say the rest.

"…that I suggested we could take the opportunity to slip away," Asher finished with a sigh, unable to look at his father. His head bowed, spilling dark hair into his face. "You know we did not wish to do it. You have no idea how many times…with all my heart, I wanted to stay."

Aidan looked at him, but said nothing. Cassiel's eyes were on the trees.

It was a strange vantage point from which to watch them, from her secret perch behind the blossoms. But as much as the princess wanted to shrink away in guilt, she was rooted to the spot.

It was like looking back through a mirror, peeling away the layers of time. The resemblance was so strong between them that the older generations could easily have been talking to a younger version of themselves. Ellanden had always been a reflection of his father, and despite the lack of blood between the vampires they seemed to favor each other more and more over time.

Perhaps that's why their parents were having such difficulty forming a reprimand. Perhaps every emotion had been blunted by shock and loss, leaving room for nothing but relief.

Perhaps they don't know everything yet.

How much had the boys told them? Did they know of the basilisk and the giant? The kelpies and the shipwreck? The wizard's enchanted cage? Would they be sitting together so peacefully in the garden if Aidan knew his son had tried to murder Cassiel's in a skeletal cavern beneath the ground?

"So that's how you did it?" Cassiel asked quietly. "You went into the water."

It was one of the first times Evie had heard her uncle speak, and the very sound of his voice tore her apart. Ellanden's eyes lifted slowly, bright with pain and grief.

"...I'm sorry."

It wasn't the first time he'd said it. It wasn't the hundredth. Each time took a little more out of him, chipping away like a dagger, piece by broken piece.

"I felt that current myself," Cassiel murmured as his mind drifted back to a memory the others would never see. "There was no way you could have survived it."

Ellanden pulled in a tight breath. "The naiads protected me."

He started to say something else, then reached for his father's hand.

It was one of the first times since he'd raced into that sunlit garden that the man had actually released him. But now the prince was the one unable to let go. He held on to him tightly, ignoring the others and murmuring in his native tongue.

But the princess was no longer watching. She was staring at the vampires instead.

While the others had clung and surrendered to each passing emotion Aidan had been consumed with a singular focus, one so relentless and overwhelming his entire body was caught in the grip of it. In the background of each conversation he remained perfectly motionless, staring at his teenage son with those wild, burning eyes. Every so often, he'd slip. Twitch compulsively forward, only to catch himself just as fast. But it was only a matter of time, before—

"*Asher.*"

The name burst out of him, like one trying to hold back the tide. Quiet enough so as not to disturb the fae, but loud enough to catch his son's attention.

There was a moment of frightening hesitation. Then—

"What you offered me before..."

Evie leaned instinctively closer for a better view. She didn't understand what he meant. She could tell Asher didn't understand either. His handsome face drew a perfect blank as he waited for further explanation. Then all at once it clicked.

...seven hells.

His lips parted with some uncertain expression, but no part of it was unkind. If anything, he was simply stunned—unable to believe his father would make such a request. It had been years since they'd spoken of such a thing. Not since he was a little boy, making a sweet and thoughtless gesture to the kind man who'd rescued him, a gesture he was still too young to fully understand.

He understood it now.

"...are you sure?"

It was the only question he ever asked. Not why. Or shouldn't we discuss this. Or perhaps more pertinently, have you lost your eternal mind? Just a simple, are you sure.

When his father didn't answer, he rolled up his sleeve.

I cannot believe this is happening.

The princess was no longer the only person who'd noticed. Ellanden had stopped talking mid-sentence and was staring in shock. Even Cassiel had broken from his trance, watching the pair with a strange expression as Asher drew in a silent breath then calmly extended his arm.

Aidan took his hand immediately, but had no plans for the wrist. He simply bit the tip of the boy's finger, kissing the hurt away, just as he'd done so many times when Asher was a child.

And just like that...it was done.

There was no way the conversation could recover. That fragile peace in the garden had been shattered beyond repair. Ellanden was secretly gawking, trying to remember what he'd been saying, while Asher was clearly shaken but trying to pretend he was fine.

Their parents had fewer tells and were far more challenging to interpret.

Considering Aidan had just forged an eternal bond with the one person on earth he'd sworn to forever protect, there had been very little change in demeanor. His eyes were cast down towards the table, dilating slightly with a rush of sensation that was only partially his own. Whatever baffling mix of emotions was plaguing Asher, his father was experiencing it tenfold.

And yet it was a different man who caught the princess' eye.

"Cada...are you not well?"

Ellanden hadn't spoken the language of his people for a long while, but having grown up in the Ivory City he rarely used the common tongue. The result was a sometimes affected pattern of speech, one that made him sound more formal than perhaps he intended.

Or perhaps that stiffness was real after all.

Cassiel opened his mouth to answer, but couldn't find the words. He was staring not at his son, but at Aidan. More specifically, at the blood on Aidan's lips. Those dark eyes zeroed in with such intensity the princess could feel it all the way on the terrace, shivering down her spine.

A strained silence fell over the garden.

"Your father is fine," Aidan replied with a tight smile. "It's your mother I worry about. She longs for your company. Why don't you go find her, Ellanden? Let your father get some rest."

Since when does the Lord of the Fae need to rest?

Ellanden pushed to his feet, deeply disturbed, but nodded obediently and headed off in search of his mother. He left the garden without a backward glance, breezing quickly inside.

But he caught the door lightly as it was swinging shut.

"Cada...I *am* sorry."

THE REST OF THE DAY passed surprisingly quickly. It seemed most everyone had spent their emotional currency at breakfast, and time was needed to recover before the next costly assault.

It was in this spirit of avoidance that Evie found herself lingering in her bedroom. Ten years she'd been missing. Ten years her parents had considered her dead. But she still had a bedroom.

She'd taken one step inside, and decided never to ask why.

"That's uncanny." Asher knocked lightly on the door frame, stepping inside at the same time. "That's the same picture you have in Taviel, isn't it? The dancers and the bear?"

She followed his gaze to the framed canvas on the wall. She'd spotted it at a carnival in Vale when she was about four—started giggling so hard, her father had purchased it on the spot.

A lifetime later, it had somehow ended up here.

"Yeah, it is." She yanked back her hair, lacing it into a quick braid. They hadn't spoken since breakfast. After what happened in the garden, he'd simply disappeared. "Where have you—"

"Here you are."

The door pushed open wider and Ellanden stepped inside. His eyes widened momentarily at the precise recreation of her bedroom, but he didn't look surprised. A chamber of his own had been waiting on the other side of the villa. He was wearing his old clothes.

"They're calling us for dinner."

Asher and Evie stared at him a moment, then nodded. Neither looked particularly inclined to gather once more in the hall. The fae was stalling as well; it's why he'd volunteered to find them.

"We could—" He caught himself before he could say more, hands digging deep into his pockets. Both eyebrows rose with an innocent shrug. "I mean, we could always..."

For the first time, Evie brightened with the hint of a smile.

"What? We could say that we're sick?'

It had never worked when they were children. She saw no hope of it working now.

Has it really come to that? Are we actively avoiding this now?

Ellanden's cheeks tinted with the hint of a blush before he bowed his head. "I suppose not."

Asher sank onto the corner of the bed, rubbing absentmindedly at the tip of his finger.

"This isn't how I thought it would be," he murmured, eyes flickering distractedly around the room. "Some things are exactly as we left, but the rest...the rest is not the same."

The other two kept silent, but agreed.

There was a heaviness to the air they didn't remember, a weight to every conversation. As if it was no longer possible to speak in the present without adding ten years of the past.

"It was never going to be normal," Ellanden offered half-heartedly. "It doesn't matter how quickly time passed for us."

It was a valid point, one they accepted without question, but the princess wasn't able to let it rest. Although the fae was quick to temper, she'd always been the one who leapt straight to rage.

"But we left for a reason," she insisted quietly, arms folded tightly across her chest. "And that same reason has brought us back." There was a slight pause. "When are we going to ask them?"

Asher lifted his head. "Ask them what?"

She perched on the mattress beside him, trying very hard not to look at his hand. "To come with us. It's the entire reason we left the fort. The entire reason we flew across the *entire* realm instead of heading straight to the Dunes to find the stone. We know who's after it now, and we know it's not a battle we can fight alone. *That's* why we're here."

Ellanden sighed quietly, leaning back against the door. "There's also the slight matter of atonement..."

"Atonement?" She turned to him sharply, voice lightening in surprise. "When did you start throwing around words like 'atonement'? You said it yourself—we did this for a *reason*—and you're the most unapologetic person I've ever met."

"And you're angry," Asher fired back. "Angry, and frightened, and it's making you cold." He and the princess might have shared a bed, but there had never been lies between them. "I'm telling you, they're not ready. You saw how they were at breakfast. It's not like they've been spending their time here sharpening swords. They've been *grieving*. And in case anyone's forgotten, they officially abdicated their thrones and divorced themselves from the five kingdoms. We're asking them to ride into battle with an army? Who's to say they'll have one to command—"

"Don't be ridiculous," Ellanden interrupted with a roll of his eyes. "You know such things are always temporary. They'll probably throw a parade when we come back—"

Evie dropped her eyes to the carpet, biting her lip. "Not the way Seth talks about it..."

"That's even more of a reason to handle this gently," Asher insisted, lowering his voice even though the people in question were half a villa away. "You weren't there this afternoon, Evie, but Landi and I had a strange encounter with them in the garden—"

"Did something else happen?" Ellanden interrupted suddenly, having worried about it the rest of the afternoon. "Did my father say something after I left?"

The vampire paused a beat, then bowed his head. "I was thinking about *my* father."

A sudden hush fell over the room.

While the boys had no way of knowing the princess had been watching from above, all three of them were remembering the same moment, just as staggered as they'd been when it happened.

"I was surprised you let him do that," Ellanden said quietly, chancing a quick glance at his friend's face. "I was even more surprised he asked you—"

"It's fine," Asher interrupted, unable to stop touching his finger. His dark eyes tensed at the memory before flickering to his girlfriend. "You won't believe me, but my father actually—"

"I know." She took his hand, stopping the manic fidgeting. "I was standing on the terrace."

There was a beat of surprise.

"Spying?" Ellanden asked incredulously.

She bristled at him, flipping the braid over her shoulder. "Not spying. Just covertly watching, with the desire to be neither seen nor heard."

"...*spying*."

"You fae are so paranoid—"

"Why are you pushing so quickly for this?" Asher squeezed her hand, reclaiming her attention. "You didn't mind stalling a few extra days so Seth could reconnect with his family. A family he'd seen only a short while before. Yet less than twenty-four hours after we arrive *here*—"

"Look around you!" She sprang to her feet and paced across the room—jamming her finger at the painting of the dancing bear. "This isn't a place they were ever intending to leave. They've put an entire map between themselves and the rest of the world. They've built themselves a home."

Not a home...a memorial.

"I cannot ask my father for such a thing," Asher countered quietly, staring down at his hands. "At least, not yet. The fact that he was actually willing to..."

He shook his head, unable to finish.

"But that's exactly my point." Evie sank down once more beside him, combing her fingers through his dark hair. "They're never going to leave this place on their own. They've dug into the very stone. And if we're not careful..."

The distant sounds of the kitchen drifted down the hall.

"I understand that things are broken. I understand that things are in need of repair." She gestured out the open window. "But this is a memory. They've been living in the clouds."

The boys said nothing, but followed her gaze.

"So when are we going to ask them?"

There was a pause. Then—

"Tomorrow," Ellanden said definitively, stepping towards the door. His mother's voice was calling down the hall and he'd be damned if he kept her waiting. "We'll ask them tomorrow."

Chapter 5

But the friends didn't ask them tomorrow. Or the next day. Or the day after that.

At first, it was easy to find excuses. They'd look for an opening, but fail to find one. They'd clear their throats in anticipation, but the words would catch on their tongues. When the excuses grew scarce, they found themselves latching on to the little things instead.

The way each of the thick candles lining the hallway stayed burning from sundown to sunrise. The way Tanya's hands started trembling every time Ellanden walked into a room. Casual tears had grown so plentiful as to go unnoticed, and while at first the princess had thought their parents were simply unarmed she now began to wonder if they didn't trust themselves with blades.

It became relatively easy to stall after that. These were the people they loved most in the world, and the things they wanted weren't unreasonable. In fact, they were shockingly simple.

They wanted time. They wanted proximity. They wanted someone to breathe light into the last ten years of darkness and simply hold their hand.

And as fate would have it...their children wanted the same thing.

There was no resisting such pure, unguarded affection. Especially when it was shared. That sense of urgency vanished by the second morning, and all further discussion was put on hold. The mountains provided a natural barrier between the rest of the world, and every time the friends even thought about leaving, to banish such thoughts they needed only to look into their parents' eyes.

It was like taking a step back in time.

They hiked together in the woods, swam together in the stream, went out each morning to pick berries they'd feast on at breakfast.

Those initial silences gave way to days of uninterrupted talking. Laughter and stories in the grassy meadows. Subtle boasting of new skills as they hunted in the woods. Wounds healed, the stiffness vanished, and those frayed nerves began to slowly repair.

Some of the greatest joy belonged to Adelaide.

While the others found themselves on a path of restoration, fixing all that had been broken, the queen's slate was already clean. Instead of mending fences she delighted in the discovery, taking that precious time to get to know the children she'd spent years painting, locked away in the woods.

There was very little common ground. There was even less shared experience. Strangely enough, one of the greatest moments of connection came when the queen was describing the recently-deceased ogre that had haunted the woods around her makeshift house.

Kailas had blinked in surprise, while Katerina asked the natural question.

"What did you name it?"

The stories came easier after that.

Freya and Seth were forcibly dragged from the periphery and embraced without question into the fold. Their reflexive deference and hesitancy to intrude was cheerfully stamped out of them, until they found themselves swept along in a sea of sparking laughter and lively discussion, warming with secret adoration as each of their childhood heroes came slowly back to life.

Of course, there were still moments of dissonance. Little cognitive splinters buried beneath all the rest. They usually came at moments of transition, when the friends were summoned inside for the evening meal or when that last flash of sunlight lit the skies over the western hills.

Each one resonated with an internal pang, like the sounding of a clock.

Time had not stopped for the rest of the realm. They could not afford to linger. And despite having surrendered to the blissful days of sunshine, they were painfully aware that all was not well.

There were specific things they *didn't* talk about. Certain subjects that were instantly silenced with the clearing of a throat or a pointed glance. Despite their isolation the doors were triple-bolted, and while the children wandered 'freely', their parents were still unable to let them out of their sight.

The lingering embraces spoke of damage, not just affection. That defensive caution sprang too quickly to their eyes. And whenever anyone made even the slightest reference to the dragon…?

All was not well. And that sunlit haven could never hope to last.

These were the thoughts troubling the princess one afternoon as she headed inside with her mother, carrying armfuls of flowers they'd picked on a mountain hike. The old blossoms had been thrown away and a fresh array of vases was already lining the top of the vanity. She watched as the famous queen deftly arranged them, staring at the back of her head with a little frown.

"Mother…what happened to Uncle Cassiel? Why is everyone so troubled for him?"

Of all the subtle improvements over the last few days, the newfound fragility in her uncle was the most reluctant to fade. It wasn't a weakness, per se. Just a profound injury that had left him so shaken, those around him quaked with phantom tremors as well.

Katerina's hands paused over the flowers.

It was impossible to deny it. It was also impossible to dissuade her headstrong daughter once she'd latched on to a question. In the end, she was left with nothing but the truth.

"Your uncle was travelling. He's only recently returned."

Evie watched her closely.

"But why—"

"He's fine…now. Aidan brought him back."

Aidan brought him back? Like a stray puppy who'd escaped its leash. Furthermore, why would the vampire have gone at all? Why would it not have been his sister? Or her own father?

She shook her head in confusion, wishing her mother would set down the flowers.

"I don't understand, what—"

"It isn't my story to tell," Katerina interrupted. "You'll have to ask one of the others."

A rather brusque dismissal, but as always the princess saw an opportunity.

"The others would never tell me," she insisted, easing between her mother and the row of vases. "They'll claim it's too personal and send me away. But you have no respect for other people's privacy. We have that in common," she added brightly, chancing a hopeful smile.

Katerina laughed under her breath, surveying her daughter.

The last few days had been a gift, but that dissonance wasn't lost on her either. The smile faded the longer she stared, taking on hues of the quiet sadness that was never far away. After a thoughtful moment, she decided that perhaps her daughter should know the story after all.

"Cassiel wasn't just travelling...he went to the Antoine Forest."

The princess shook her head blankly. "What is—"

"It's where his people go to die."

Her mouth fell open in absolute shock. If given a hundred years, she never would have guessed such a thing. It was baffling enough that the Fae had such a place, but that her uncle would have gone there himself? How had the others allowed it to happen? What about Tanya?

"I can't believe that," she gasped, tears filling her eyes. "How can you even...?" She trailed off faintly, wishing she'd never opened her mouth. "Why would he do such a thing?"

For a moment the sun itself seemed to diminish, leaving her mother's face shadowed and cold. She realized now, it always looked like that. Fleeting smiles could never warm it for long.

"He lost his only child, Everly. And unlike the rest of us, he would be cursed to live with that pain forever. In a way, it's ironic Aidan was the one to find him. He followed their bond."

Evie took a step back, so dizzied with emotion it was a wonder she didn't fall over.

This wasn't the time for soft-spoken truths. It was a time for shock and screaming. How could her mother say such a thing so calmly? As if there was something rational in it, as if there was an absence of choice. The fae had just recently returned? She hadn't even set down the blossoms!

"Father must have been furious," she rallied, latching on to the most insignificant part.

"He wasn't," Katerina answered softly. She considered a moment, then amended, "He slept outside Cass' door for a month, but he wasn't angry."

Evie's breath quickened, as if the walls themselves were closing in. "*You* must have been furious. How could Cassiel even consider it?"

The seconds passed quietly between them.

Please say you were furious. Please say you don't understand.

Her mother stared at her a moment longer, then stepped past to continue with the flowers. That terrible air of calm never left her, but her shoulders drooped with a silent sigh.

"Sweetheart...I pray you always ask that question. I pray you never come to know such a feeling yourself. Never in my life have I been so grateful for my own mortality. Just knowing it would eventually end...sometimes, it was the only thing that got me through the day."

She finished with the blossoms, turning back around.

"Cassiel didn't have that. He was facing an eternity with a broken heart. In a matter of years his wife would die as well, leaving him completely alone for the rest of time."

Her eyes tightened and she took her daughter's hand.

"...would you not have done the same?"

EVIE LEFT HER MOTHER soon after, wandering the sunlit halls and shivering against a chill that had settled into her very bones. She paused ever so slightly as she passed the door to Cassiel and Tanya's room. For one of the first times, it was closed. Soft voices were talking on the other side.

She hesitated a few seconds, then headed out to the garden.

It was easier to breathe in the open air, losing herself in the familiar scent of honeysuckle and jasmine. Neither one was particularly in season, yet they'd both somehow managed to bloom.

"Did you have a nice time with your mother?"

She glanced up suddenly, to see Asher sitting by himself on one of the garden benches. The exact same bench where his father had taken his blood just a few days before. A soft glow of late-morning sunlight illuminated his pale features and a handful of white petals had fallen into his hair.

She sank onto the bench in front of him, leaning back into his chest.

"I can't get over it," she murmured, eyes drifting around the house. "The way it looks just like the one in Taviel."

It was one of those forbidden subjects they'd never mentioned, how in the world their parents had managed to construct such a thing in the middle of a mountain pass. As if the building itself wasn't enough, there were the materials. Had they carried each one up, piece by piece?

"It looks like Taviel," he agreed softly, "but it feels like a tomb. A tomb of our best memories...though none of them happened here."

Sounds like someone else had a difficult morning.

Instead of asking, she glanced down at his hands—endlessly fiddling with his finger.

"I still can't believe you bonded with your father."

He caught himself at the same time, then wrapped his arms deliberately around her waist. It was the first time they'd done such a thing since leaving the fort. They closed their eyes for a moment and pulled in a breath, silently reveling in the mere proximity.

"If only I'd done it sooner," he murmured, eyes clouding in thought. "Then none of this might have happened—"

"That's not why he did it now," she interrupted, glancing over her shoulder.

He was smart enough to realize this and didn't dispute it. He just nodded with that same pensive frown, lifting his eyes to the distant peaks. The mountains stretched out endlessly in every direction. As a dragon, it had seemed infinitely more manageable. As a girl...she was overwhelmed.

"You had offered once before?" she prompted curiously.

She already knew that he had. He'd told her years ago. But details had always been scarce.

He nodded silently, hugging her tighter to his chest.

"Not long after he rescued me."

There was a hitch in his breathing. They hadn't spoken of the tragedy that had befallen his clan, but she knew it weighed heavy on his mind. Perhaps rescued was no longer the correct word.

"I remember wandering into his study," he continued quietly, "climbing onto his lap without a word and holding out my arm." His lips curved with the ghost of a smile. "I hadn't really given it much thought. It just felt like I should. It was...it was the first time I ever called him my father."

Evie froze in his arms, eyes fixed on the jasmine.

He used to call him Aidan. I'd forgotten that.

"He turned me down," he concluded with a short laugh. "He knew that I didn't understand what I was actually offering." Without seeming to think about it, he reached again for the tip of his finger. "I'm not sure he understood what he was asking now..."

She twisted around, staring up at him. "But you let him do it anyway."

He took a measured breath, then nodded. "He's my father."

They stayed like that a moment longer, then she turned forward once again and leaned into his arms. Timing out her own breaths with the steady rise and fall of his chest.

"I miss you," she murmured, not realizing how much it had been weighing on her until she said the words out loud. "It seems ridiculous to be in the same house...but not in the same bed."

He nodded again, pressing a soft kiss to the back of her head.

"These last few days, it's like being a child again." He gazed over the balcony, resting his cheek on her hair. "But we're not children anymore. That time has passed."

Yes, it has.

Instead of pursuing this further, instead of making any concrete plans, they lapsed back into silence—each staring into the distance, lost in thought. The sun drifted in a slow orbit above them, but despite the number of people packed into the house they weren't disturbed.

When the princess finally spoke again, he startled at the sound.

"My father did the same thing."

He glanced down at her.

"...what?"

She shrugged in a resigned sort of way.

"He drank some of my blood as well. Wasn't really my decision, but these things are usually spur of the moment." She let out a martyred sigh. "Now we are forever bound..."

His chest shook in silent laughter as he gave her a punishing squeeze.

"Why must you always be so horrid? You make it sound like a cult."

"It *absolutely* is."

"Then why did you volunteer?" he teased. "You didn't seem to mind so much back at the fort. As I recall, you rather enjoyed yourself..."

His hand drifted below her jaw, angling her face gently towards him. That had always been his way, little coaxing gestures. Sweet and transparent. Paired with an irresistible smile.

So much time we wasted. How did I not love him sooner?

"I can hardly remember," she whispered, just an inch away from his lips. "Perhaps we can steal away into the forest. You can help remind me—"

"Evie?"

The two sprang away from each other as Dylan rounded the corner, breezing into the garden with a charismatic smile. Under any other circumstances, it would have been impossible to hide their affection. The man had once banished an insufferable lieutenant whose son had danced too closely to the princess at a celebratory ball. But on that particular morning the king's thoughts were elsewhere, and he only had eyes for his daughter.

"You're finally back." He lit up at the very sight of her, the same way he'd done since the moment she'd arrived. "Your mother stole you long enough. I demand the same opportunity." His eyes twinkled as he cocked his head towards the mountain trail. "Care for a walk?"

She pushed immediately to her feet. "Of course. 'Bye, Ash."

The vampire watched them depart with a secret smile.

"No blood-letting, you two."

Dylan glanced over his shoulder with a frown. "What did he say?"

Evie steered him forward, biting the inside of her cheek. "It's nothing."

<hr />

AS SOON AS THEY WERE beyond the villa's gates the pair left the trail behind and forged their own path, weaving their way through the foliage and into the woods. It had been the same way since the princess was just a child, to the eternal chagrin of her mother. Perhaps it was ranger's influence, but her father had never subscribed to royal protocol when it came to raising his daughter.

He knew how to live off the land...she would, too.

He roasted squirrels over an open fire...she would, too.

"You've really been out here gathering flowers this whole time?" He slowed his pace the second they lost sight of the villa, as if some part of him felt caged by it as well. "I can't fathom how either of you possibly stayed awake."

She fell into step beside him, soft pine needles crunching beneath her feet.

"They brighten the place up. It needs a little brightening," she added with a sideways glance.

No matter how hard she tried not to she couldn't stop imagining him wrapped in a blanket, sleeping on the floor outside his best friend's door.

He shot her a quick look, then pushed ahead with a deliberate smile. "Come on—there's something I want to show you."

For the next half-mile they wandered through a sunlit pattern of hollyhock and juniper, redwood and pine. Conversation gave way to long stretches of companionable silence, filled with the sounds of the forest, the same untamed descant that had scored so many of their walks in the past.

This was my classroom. This is where he taught me everything I know.

For longer than the princess could remember, her father had done everything in his power to make the woods a second home. Some of her first memories were of exactly such a scene, riding on his shoulders and listening to the smooth cadence of his voice as he narrated the world around them, pointing out a thousand little details she would never have otherwise seen.

By the time she was five she knew the best places to make a shelter, the fastest way to locate water, how to start a fire when left with nothing but damp wood. She recognized the different bird songs, and knew which animals to follow in times of danger and which poisonous plants to avoid.

Most importantly, he'd taught her to follow the stars.

In case you ever get lost, he'd murmured, pointing up at them. *You can find your way back home.*

"This is it."

The princess stopped abruptly, not realizing where they were standing until she felt the spray of water upon her face. They'd been hiking down a steady slope towards the valley, following the slight curve of a river that had suddenly vanished, plunging a hundred feet in a magnificent cascade.

"It's beautiful," she murmured, stepping closer on the slick stone.

It was impossible to see the bottom from such a distance, only the swirling clouds of mist where the rushing water crashed into the distant stream. She could feel it, though. Even from such a great height, those pounding vibrations rattled up through her feet.

"It's the reason I picked this place," Dylan answered, steadying her with an unseen hand.

She glanced back in surprise. "*You* picked it?"

Ever since she and the others had learned of their parents' departure, she'd always imagined her father was the one fighting against it. That more than everyone else, he'd want to stay.

He nodded silently, hands in his pockets. "It was the only thing that was moving. The only thing that made noise. Everywhere else they wanted to build...it was so quiet and still."

She froze a split second, then stole a quick glance.

On the surface, he had the same look as the rest of them—unspeakably relieved, but with a profound sense of weariness that seemed to resonate in his very soul. He was in stasis, confined to the lovely borders of this place he'd apparently chosen...but there was something else there as well.

A restless energy humming below the surface. An unquenchable spark of adventure stirring in his eyes. It was hard to see. After so much time, it had almost faded completely. But it was there.

And it was the only hope the princess had.

"This actually reminds me of cliff-diving with Seth," she said abruptly, pretending not to notice when he glanced over in surprise. "We shifted with the rest of his pack and were running through the forest. I thought the run was the highlight, but they had this crazy tradition of leaping straight off the side of a mountain. I was a little hesitant to try it myself...needed a little push."

He was facing her now, the waterfall forgotten.

"Seth pushed you? He pushed you off a cliff?"

Big mistake.

Young shifters were known to get carried away on occasion. As one of the worst offenders, her father was usually more indulgent than most. But that leniency did not extend to his daughter.

"I jumped," she clarified quickly, lying only a little. "We jumped together. I've never done anything like that. It was pure adrenaline. I'd never even gotten to run with a pack..."

Her father went very still beside her, staring with an expression she'd never quite seen. It warmed him from the inside out, edged with a desperate kind of longing before retreating quickly.

"I wish I had seen that," he said softly, turning back to the falls.

She stepped deliberately between him and the falls.

No more stalling. No more dodging.

No more pretending we have infinite time.

"It was nothing," she breathed, staring up into his eyes. "It was nothing compared to our trek through Aluthan's Hammer. Or the time we had to fight a herd of kelpies, or steal a ship from a horde of Carpathians, or found ourselves trapped inside that sorcerer's cave."

A silent look passed between them.

"There are things I need to tell you."

It was a moment of reckoning, and for a few terrifying seconds she was worried he wasn't ready to hear. Ten years of bleeding couldn't resolve overnight. There was a reason they were having this conversation on the top of a mountain, hundreds of miles from the rest of the world.

Then again...perhaps this had been his plan all along.

Taking his daughter to a place that was shielded by the forest, muffled by the sound of the falls. A place where the others wouldn't find them, where they could speak freely, with no illusions or forced smiles. A place to reveal all those dark secrets, without the weight of her mother's tears.

"...Father?"

The world around them blurred out of focus as they stood in silence—poised on the edge of something much larger than themselves. Another look passed between them. One the princess knew she'd remember for the rest of her life. Then he made a quiet decision and pulled in a breath.

"Tell me."

Just like that, the floodgates opened.

The stories rushed out of her in a breathless jumble, stringing nonsensically together, each coming faster than the last. From the witch to the basilisk, from the shipwreck to the Kreo, from their detour into an enchanted swamp, to the band of slavers that tried to kidnap her and Ellanden on the side of the road. The pack of undead leopards that had chased them across the tundra, the bloody skirmish in the grasslands, their race through the giant's garden after escaping that fiery cage.

Piece by piece she recounted the fantastical story, taking him along on the journey, stitching together each convoluted tale, until at last they reached the inevitable conclusion.

Standing on the edge of another cliff. Wondering whether to jump.

Her father had listened in perfect silence, committing each detail to memory, unaware that from the moment she'd started talking he had been holding his breath.

By the time it was over, tears were running freely down his face.

"This prophecy…what does it say?"

She squared her shoulders and recited those fateful words said at the carnival so many years ago. Maybe she should have told him then. Maybe things had happened exactly as they were meant to. At the end of the day, it no longer mattered. She supposed they would never know.

He was quiet for a long time after she finished, staring at the crashing falls. The man was no stranger to the fates, having surrendered himself to the will of a prophecy long ago.

But that didn't make it any easier now.

"Three shall set out…though three shall not return."

I was kind of hoping to gloss over that part.

She stood there in silence, unsure what to say. But her father didn't seem to require her to say anything at all. He simply stood there, regarding her with a thoughtful frown.

"…and still you went?"

Their eyes met for a suspended moment.

"I am my father's daughter."

Chapter 6

Evie didn't wait for another transition. She didn't wait for another sunset. She marched out of the forest and straight back to the villa, determined not to waste another day.

The rest of them had settled in the garden, soaking up the rays of a balmy afternoon sun.

For just a split second that momentum stalled and she was struck with a strange feeling of suspension, just as she'd had the night it all started, perched on the windowsill outside Ellanden's room. Such a peaceful, heartwarming picture. It seemed a small tragedy to disturb.

Tanya was breezing back and forth from the kitchen, clinging to her newfound role of hostess with both hands. She paused behind Asher's chair and tapped the point of his nose, leaning down and muttering something that made him laugh. She pressed a warm glass into his hand a second later. If she'd been up at dawn massacring mountain goats, he wouldn't have been surprised.

Freya and Cosette were perched on the stone railing next to Adelaide, listening to the queen's stories as one braided flowers into the other's hair. Serafina and Kailas were at a nearby table, pretending not to listen but glancing up every so often with the same twinkling smile.

In a rather unlikely pairing, Seth and Aidan were playing a game of cards.

The young shifter had been nothing short of terrified of the vampire when he'd first arrived, keeping an instinctual barrier of distance and secretly panicking every time they were left in the same room. An eventual exception had been made for Asher, but every child born of the five kingdoms had the same ingrained fear. It had been tragically reinforced and was nearly impossible to unlearn.

Fortunately, the vampire in question had infinite patience.

In only a few days' time, Aidan had won the boy over. Perhaps it was that innately soothing way about him. Perhaps it was his centuries of practice, making people see past the fangs.

It helped that he was letting Seth win.

There was only a hint of friction. A cool distance had sprung up between Ellanden and his father. They were sitting on opposite sides of the garden, avoiding each other's eyes.

Evie glanced curiously between them as her own father gave her a quick squeeze.

Are you ready?

He didn't actually ask the question, the same way he hadn't said a word in the forest after she'd concluded her astonishing tale. He'd heard the words of the prophecy. He knew what steps came next. And even though he'd give his life for her *not* to take them, he'd learned long ago the futility of fighting against one's destiny. He would stand with her. He would not stand in her way.

She cleared her throat and took a step forward.

"These last few days have been a dream…but it's time for us to go."

A hushed silence fell over the garden.

The cards came down, the hands went still, the conversation paused, still hanging on their lips. Even the sun knew better than to make itself known, ducking politely behind a wisp of cloud as the princess stood at the center of it all, trembling under the weight of those piercing gazes.

"We thought we'd never see you again," she forced herself onward. "We truly didn't think we'd get the chance. So many nights we spent longing for this very moment, a part of me never wants to leave. All of us gathered together…this is my heaven."

She stared at them a moment longer before shaking her head.

"But it isn't real."

An invisible shockwave rippled across the garden.

Cassiel shot a quick look at his son, but for one of the first times Ellanden was beyond his reach. Serafina and Kailas paled with the same stricken expression, while Aidan was gripping the table hard enough that little cracks appeared in the side. There was a quiet intake of breath as Katerina ghosted unnoticed onto the terrace, watching the scene unfold from above.

"We were given a prophecy," Evie continued quietly, unable to bear looking at any person in particular. "We were tasked with the safety of the entire realm. That carries a responsibility that outweighs any personal feelings we might have ourselves. No matter how desperate—"

"No."

The others were reeling, but that had never suited the Kreo queen. She set down the pitcher with an icy expression, joining the princess in the center of the shaded square.

Evie's pulse skittered unevenly as she tried to stand her ground. "I'm not saying this to hurt you. But it has to be done—"

"Then let someone else do it," the woman interrupted shortly. "We have been down this road before, throwing ourselves against some cosmic mandate until there weren't pieces big enough left to break. I have lost enough to the words of a prophecy. Let this one fall to someone else—"

"This one *did* fall to someone else," Dylan interrupted quietly, standing in the entryway behind his daughter. "We have not been tasked with this, Tanya. It was given to the children."

She took a step back, staring in astonishment. "I can't believe what I'm hearing."

"Hang on—"

"This from the man who tore the five kingdoms apart searching for his daughter!" she cried indignantly. "The man who banished his beloved mentor and razed entire villages to the ground!"

Evie flinched at the venom in her voice, thinking painfully of Michael.

"We *just* got them back, Dylan! And you would allow this—"

"It's not a matter of me allowing it," he replied evenly, tempering her wild anger with deliberate calm. "This is a *prophecy*. Slightly beyond my jurisdiction. I'm only saying you cannot forbid such a thing just because it happens to involve your son."

Her eyes flashed in the flickering light.

"Watch me."

At this point Evie melted back nervously, wondering if the two of them might actually come to blows. In all her time spent imagining this moment, never would she have thought things could unravel so far. But her grandmother was right. Never had she known unspeakable pain.

Her father took a simultaneous step forward, staring at the volatile shifter with nothing but an aching tenderness in his eyes. How many times had she clung to him these last years, weeping uncontrollably over the loss of her son? How many times had she found him wandering the woods, listening to his breathless rants and rages before he broke down and did the same thing?

"It's their time, Tanya." He spoke softly, but each word carried across the stone. "It's their destiny. Who are we to stand in their way?"

Evie's eyes flew up in shock, fastening on the back of his head. Many times she'd heard her father speak about such things, but it was almost always done as a punchline. If not that, it was said merely to infuriate the fae. Never had she heard the note of quiet deference in his voice.

She didn't know what to make of it. Neither did Tanya.

The tiny queen paused for a split second, then cast a look at her son.

"We're their parents," she snapped, unwilling to discuss it further. "Now, if there is some new darkness descending upon the land, we'll fight it back ourselves—"

"Right," Ellanden muttered under his breath.

She trailed off in shock as Cassiel looked at him sharply.

"Ellanden."

"No—I'm tired of apologizing for this." The fae pushed to his feet, unable to stomach the sunlit garden a second longer. "Everly is right. We were given a prophecy. We left to fulfill it. We had to do so in secret, because there was no way you would have allowed us to go. Then, before we could even start, we were kidnapped by a sorcerer and held prisoner for ten years."

He glared across the patio, daring anyone to disagree.

"I'm looking hard at what we've done, Father. I see nothing wrong. I see no need to apologize to you or anyone else. But you...you have a lot to answer for."

This time it was Evie who stopped him quickly, remembering the heartbreaking story her mother had told just a few hours before. "Landi, don't—"

"Let him speak," Cassiel said quietly, staring back at him. "For what must I answer?"

The prince threw out his hands, gesturing to the lovely villa.

"What is this place?" he demanded. "Why are you here? How can you possibly live with yourselves, hiding away in the mountains while the rest of the realm suffers without relief?"

He looked at each of them in turn, seething with quiet rage.

"Perhaps the fates foretold such weakness," he finished coldly. "Perhaps this is why the prophecy was given to us instead—"

"Ellanden!"

This time so many people said it, it was impossible to know which ones got through. But Asher was the one to push to his feet, stepping deliberately between the fae and his father.

"You may be right, but do not be cruel," he said under his breath, just loud enough for his friend to hear. "You will not be able to live with yourself come morning."

"Why do you defend them?" the fae countered, yanking his arm free. "You feel the same as I do, Asher. Yet you're content to bide your time here, while Kaleb Grey searches for the stone—"

"Kaleb Grey," Kailas interrupted in a low murmur, saying his little brother's name for the first time. His eyes flashed instinctively to the terrace, finding his twin amongst the leaves. "He is our blood, our responsibility. We should be the ones to stop him—"

"Yet you were not called upon to do so," Evie interrupted sharply, wondering why he was staring with such intensity into the trees. "And lest you forget... he is my blood, too. And you're not the only one who can turn into a dragon."

Aidan leaned back slowly in his chair, looking her up and down.

"So now it is a matter of skill?" he asked quietly. "Then why did you come here, Evie? When you know the people in this garden far surpass your own?"

He didn't say it to provoke or demean. There was genuine curiosity in the words. Better than that, it allowed her the opportunity to make their fateful request.

"Because I've seen the dragon," she answered directly, squaring her shoulders as the peripheral conversations came to a sudden halt. "I've dreamt of him since leaving the castle. Bigger and more ferocious than Kailas and my mother combined. I just didn't know his name."

More than anything else she'd said, *this* produced a reaction.

Adelaide bowed her head, while her own companions stiffened grimly. But it was their parents who were far more telling. The news didn't crush or subdue, it brought them back to life.

Tanya abandoned her aggressive posture immediately, staring towards the western peaks with a look that was both collected and appraising. Cassiel and Dylan exchanged a communicative glance, while Aidan lifted his eyes with a thoughtful expression that didn't quite hide the edge.

There was a quite fluttering of jasmine as Katerina came down from the terrace.

"You dreamt of him?" she repeated softly, looking into her daughter's eyes.

Evie nodded slowly, holding her gaze.

"What did the dragon do?" Aidan asked with that quiet intensity.

She shivered involuntarily, remembering the look in those soulless eyes.

"He rose up out of the sand, laughed at me. Told me we were going to be too late." She pulled in a deep breath. "Then he shot off towards the High Kingdom...to burn it to the ground."

Kailas rose slowly from his chair while her mother remained perfectly still, staring towards the horizon with a very particular look in her eyes. It was one thing to be driving back a never-ending onslaught of unbiased evil. It was quite another when that evil had a name and a voice.

When it was targeting the place they used to call home.

"Katerina?"

Since striking off so many years ago on an adventure of their own, Dylan Hale had been the unofficial leader of their parents' group. The one the rest of them turned to. The one whose opinion guided the direction of the rest. But throughout everything, there was one person that *he* turned to.

He was looking for her decision now.

Please...please let this work...

"It sounds like you'll need an army to fight this dragon." Katerina turned to her daughter, eyes still flickering with that deadly fire. "Quite possibly several armies."

"And a few dragons," Kailas added with a faint smile.

"Most definitely a few dragons," her mother answered quietly, turning her gaze once more towards the horizon. "It sounds like we'll need to tear him straight out of the sky..."

Freya leaned forward covertly, whispering into Seth's ear. "This is awesome."

"Keep it together."

"You'll have to officially un-ground me." Cosette hopped off the balcony with a bright smile, shaking the trailing jasmine from her hair. "It was hilarious that you tried, but it's much better this way. Now we can go monster-hunting together."

Kailas shot a pained smile towards the heavens, while Serafina pushed lightly to her feet.

"It's hardly original, is it?" she quipped. "Drive back the darkness, save the realm."

Aidan chuckled quietly, laying a winning hand upon the table.

"It's a rite of passage. Unite the four kingdoms. Do it using a stone."

"Five kingdoms," Asher corrected softly, throwing a look at his father. "There are still five."

Evie watched breathlessly as the rest of them pushed to their feet. Considering how long they'd been secluding themselves atop a mountain, they were remarkably eager to leave.

Especially considering what was waiting for them.

"So this is really happening?" she asked, almost to herself. "You'll really come?"

The others were already filtering quickly out of the garden, sweeping into the villa to gather what supplies they needed. Speaking quietly amongst themselves about what steps came next.

After casting a silent look at the others, Aidan headed off into the forest to unearth the stash of weapons he'd buried the day they first arrived.

"Of course we're coming," Dylan answered softly, squeezing her against his chest in a one-armed hug. "After so many years, did you honestly think I'd let you out of my sight?"

She laughed in spite of herself, wiping an unexpected tear from her cheek.

"I just…I can't believe it. I wasn't lying, what I said before." Her breath caught and she leaned against him with a sudden shiver. "I really didn't think we'd ever make it back."

Her parents exchanged a quick look over the top of her head.

"But you did," Katerina said simply. "And now it's time to finish this."

Dylan caught her eye with a little smile. "Better than that…it's time to go home."

Chapter 7

When one had spent their childhood living in various castles throughout the realm, home could mean a great many places. But in this case, her father had meant it quite literally.

They were going to Belaria. The closest kingdom to where they were now.

Evie was *thrilled*.

Despite having spent more time growing up in the High Kingdom, there had always been a special place in her heart for the wolves of her father's native land. The Belarian high court could be as formal and decadent as the next, but there was something delightfully primal about it as well.

The windows were always open. The aristocracy trained in the same sparring ring as the guards. Royal celebrations and other long-winded events were often held outdoors.

Best of all was the restless inability to stay human.

The princess couldn't count how many times one of her tutors would grow just as tired of the lesson as their students, declare a spontaneous 'recess', and lead them all on a romp through the woods. It was a universal impulse, one that affected the courtiers and townsfolk alike. Every morning growing up she would drag over a footstool and stand on her tiptoes to reach the window, watching excitedly as the pack who'd spent the night patrolling blurred past the castle wall.

It was a rite of passage she'd always watched from a distance. The gift of her people stirring in her blood. How many times had she pressed her face to the glass, desperate to join them?

And now...I finally can.

"Knock, knock!"

She glanced around as her mother popped her head inside the open doorway, holding a leather satchel in her hands. She was wearing a weathered travelling cloak and looking brighter than she had in almost a decade, but her eyes tightened upon finding her daughter in the center of the room.

"So strange to actually see you in here," she murmured, blinking swiftly, as if not quite trusting her own eyes. "You have no idea how many times I'd..."

Evie tensed apprehensively, then moved them deliberately past it.

"What's in the bag?"

Katerina glanced down quickly, grateful for the reprieve.

"Weapons," she said bluntly, pulling open the top to allow a glimpse inside. "Knives mostly, but there are a few other pieces. I wasn't sure what you brought with you."

Nothing like the quality you'd have here.

The princess rushed forward eagerly, taking the parcel from her hands. "These are great—thank you!"

Each one was carefully wrapped and clean. Already sharpened and ready to be pulled out at a moment's notice. Even the knots were made to be easily broken.

She recognized the ranger's careful hands.

"Does Father know you're giving these to me?" she asked with sudden suspicion.

Katerina froze with a flash of guilt, then shook her head with a grin.

"No...and I prefer you didn't tell him. He can be so sensitive about this kind of thing."

The princess chuckled and nodded, slipping the parcel into her pack. Considering they'd never planned on leaving, there were certainly plenty of things already primed to go. Packs, tents, dried goods, and flasks. It was as though they'd simply been waiting for someone to open the door.

"I won't. And thanks again."

Katerina pressed her fingers to her lips in a parting kiss then slipped into the hall with a fixed smile, moving quickly back to her own room before her daughter could see her cry.

Perfect, Evie thought to herself, taking stock. *Then I have weapons, clothes, boots, coin—*

"Almost packed?"

She whipped around to see her father in the same doorway where her mother had stood a second before. He was staring with the same bright smile, determined *not* to look around the room.

"I'm guarding them," she joked, reassessing the pile. "Can never be too careful."

"On that note..." Dylan glanced quickly up and down the hall before slipping inside and extracting something from his pocket, pressing a pair of daggers into her hands. "I know you can use these, but I'm hoping you won't have to." He looked at her seriously, tucking a lock of hair behind her ear. "This isn't going to be how it was before—with the six of you scraping by on your own. As soon as we reach Belaria, we'll continue on with a royal guard. This is just a precaution."

"Just a precaution," she echoed quickly, slipping the daggers into her pack. "Although, for the record, we weren't scraping by. We happen to have done magnificently."

She expected him to make a joke. There were certainly plenty of jokes to be made. But he didn't. Instead, he nodded slowly—looking her up and down.

"Yes, you did. Taking down a horde of Carpathians with a pair of wolves and a handful of arrows?" His eyes twinkled with a little smile. "I can't say I'm surprised. But I'm impressed."

She blushed immediately, pleased beyond words. "Yes, well...that was mostly Ellanden, pretending to be a lunatic entrepreneur." She rolled her eyes for good measure. "As you can imagine, it wasn't exactly a stretch."

He let out a sparkling laugh, sweeping back his hair. "The fae have always been more deranged than they care to admit. When this is all over, we'll make a concerted effort to get them some professional assistance."

She nodded solemnly as he crossed back to the door. "Probably best to spring it on them. They're usually armed as well."

He nodded with a grin, but paused suddenly in the doorway—glancing back at the blades he'd just given his daughter. "Speaking of...I'd prefer if you didn't tell your mother. She can be so sensitive about this kind of thing."

Evie gave a valiant salute, then turned back to her bed with a secret smile.

Parents...

Having officially claimed the nostalgic shrine as a bedroom left her in the unique position of packing her own belongings from a place she'd never technically seen. She couldn't begin to imagine the psychological toll of bringing each item to the mountain, recreating her childhood room.

The finished effect was too sparse and sad to be functional. Too empty to do anything but cause unspeakable amounts of pain. But that still left a few things she could pack.

"Oh, I love this..."

With eager fingers, she reached onto a bookshelf and uncorked a bottle of her favorite perfume. She'd gotten it from a street fair not long before the night of the carnival, a tincture of freesia and jasmine. It was half-empty, though she remembered it to be nearly full.

Another flash of dissonance. She carefully placed it back on the shelf.

"Preening, are we?"

She looked up with a grin as Freya waltzed into the room. Unlike the rest of them, the witch had nothing personal to pack. But that hadn't stopped her from pilfering all she could from Cosette.

"And you're kissing up to the fae," she replied, gesturing to the girl's traditional dress. The pale silk and gossamer sleeves draped her thin frame like a dream. "You think that's going to stop the rest of the High Born from noticing their prince is dating a witch? Might want to invest in some prosthetics. Or you could just get drunk and let Ash and me try to point your ears…"

She trailed off in surprise, looking at the girl's stricken expression.

"What's wrong?"

For perhaps the first time in her life, the lovely witch was speechless. The smile was gone and that irrepressible sparkle in her eyes had been replaced with a look of honest shock.

"Their prince…" she repeated slowly, trying it out for size. "I'd never really…" She trailed off, staring at the gown with a look of deep concern. "That had never mattered until now."

Evie sobered immediately, adjusting her own expression, but couldn't quite manage to hide her surprise. "But you're always joking about us being royalty—"

"Because we're usually traveling in a bog," she said bluntly. "The fact that you were born in a castle makes it a lot funnier when you're drenched in mud. But I always…separated them."

By now concern had turned to utter misery, and she wanted quite badly to throw the dress away. She fidgeted helplessly with the sleeves, feeling abruptly ridiculous to be wearing it at all.

"We were nowhere near Taviel," she murmured softly. "And to be frank, the odds of us reaching it were never that great. Landi and I had never even kissed before a few days ago. We'd been dancing around it all this time. And now that we're finally together…"

Evie softened and reached for her hand.

"…he's the prince again."

"Yeah."

"…and he loves you."

"Yeah."

There was a beat of silence.

"I'm going to change out of this dress."

She slipped out the door just as Cosette came inside, knocking the fae backwards in her haste to leave. There was a sharp crack of the head, followed by, "I know you stole that, you little wretch," before the woodland princess hopped lightly onto the bed, folding her legs beneath her.

"We're going to have to do something about that one."

Evie stared at the open doorway with a frown. "Yeah, we are..."

Cosette glanced up curiously. "I meant *stab* her. What are you talking about?"

Fortunately, the princess was spared having to answer as the sound of a fierce argument echoed suddenly down the hall. The girls shared a grin as two voices shot back and forth, both so utterly exasperated they didn't seem to realize they were drifting between different languages.

"—toin ci mahret and control your damn temper—"

"Alias tegalin!" Ellanden fired back, pacing swiftly towards the door. "As if you didn't think the exact same thing. At least I had the courage to say it, sial tos mor—"

There was an echoing slap.

"Apologize."

A beat of silence.

"...sorry."

They appeared in the doorway a second later, flashing cursory smiles that immediately faded as they began to suspect they'd been overheard. The shining mark on the fae's cheek didn't help.

"Hey," he greeted as he slipped inside, turning casually to hide it, "are you about finished packing? I think they want to head off before it gets dark."

Such a hurry, Evie thought with secret delight. *You'd think they were eager to go.*

"I still don't understand the need to pack," Asher murmured, his eyes lingering on the same bottle of perfume. "Not if we could just fly directly to the capital."

"We *can't* fly directly to the capital," Cosette said patiently. "I keep trying to tell you, things are not the same as when you left. A dragon crosses unannounced into Belarian borders, they'd shoot it right out of the sky. Not to mention...this is happening pretty fast for them." Her dark eyes drifted thoughtfully to the window, as if she could see faces on the other side. "Let them camp in the woods a few nights. Gather their thoughts, catch their breath. They've been here a long time."

Evie caught a whiff of freesia and jasmine.

Yes, they have.

The room darkened a shade, as if reflecting their thoughts, and the fae princess shook her head with a gentle smile, looking at each one in turn.

"I don't think there's a way you can understand it...the *shock* of seeing you alive. There's not just relief, or wonder, or even happiness...it is a *shocking* thing to see you standing there."

She trailed off thoughtfully, eyes drifting back in time.

"That's how it was for me. The moment I found you...it was like a dream I'd been having had suddenly come to life. I just pulled back the curtain and there you were." She laughed shortly. "I thought for a moment, maybe the sorcerer's magic had worked after all."

She pulled in another breath, then shook her head. "I'm glad we stayed here a few days. I'm glad you gave them some time." She glanced at Asher with a faint smile. "Especially your father. He needed it."

Ellanden looked up in surprise. "*His* father? Mine was incapable of speech."

Her lovely smile turned rather grim. "And his stopped feeding."

What?!

"What?!" Asher echoed immediately, staring in alarm. "A vampire can't just stop drinking blood...it's impossible. They'd go mad."

"He already was mad, Asher," she answered softly. "I don't think he even noticed."

Another silence fell between them. This one was even harder than the first. In a flash, those perfumed flowers grew almost overwhelming. Evie looked to the window, wanting to throw it open.

"But that's over now. It's in the past."

Cosette pushed lightly to her feet, determined to soften those difficult truths as best she could. She swept across the room to the bookshelf before pulling down a worn copy of fables. The dragon on the cover had been touched so many times the edges were beginning to fade.

"You used to read me this, do you remember?" She pressed it into Asher's hand, then stretched onto her toes and tapped her forehead lightly to his. "We used to do that, too."

The others watched as the vampire melted on the spot. His lips parted with such a rush of feeling, it threatened to overwhelm. Then he nodded slowly, eyes on her rosy cheeks.

"...I remember."

She flashed a little smile, flicking the cover of the book.

"Keep that, would you? We can read it again in Taviel."

The breathtaking fae left a moment later, leaving her three friends rooted to the spot. They stared after her in silence, seeing through the nostalgia to the light on the other side.

It was like coming up for air. But it brought some questions at the same time.

"There are *five* kingdoms," Ellanden quoted, catching his friend's eye. "What are you going to tell your father about the vampires?"

Evie glanced between them, waiting for the answer herself.

Their parents knew that vampires had burned the Kreo village. They knew the friends had been somehow left alive. But that was the extent of it. She wasn't sure Asher had even mentioned the clan in question answered to Diana, let alone their secret dwelling inside the mountain.

"I'm not sure yet," the vampire murmured thoughtfully, staring down at the bed. "I made a promise to Diana before we left...a promise I'm reluctant to break."

Who are you protecting with that promise? The vampires...or us?

The others stared at him in silence, both wondering the same thing. Then they glanced at each other and decided to keep those questions forever to themselves.

"It's a lot of secrets we've kept," Ellanden said instead, stealing a canteen from the princess' bag before pacing to the door. "I'd be careful keeping any more of them."

<hr />

EVIE HAD ASSUMED SHE'D be the one flying. She was shocked to realize she was not.

"Kailas," she scoffed, breathing with secret relief when she saw the rather large group of people and supplies. "Why must it be Kailas? I'm perfectly capable of doing it myself."

The entire group had gathered atop the same rooftop where she and her friends had landed just a few days earlier, assessing the things they'd brought in soft voices while Kailas prepared to depart. There had been a rather spirited disagreement regarding several cases of whiskey, but things had quieted down and the time was nearly upon them.

Not a moment too soon.

The sun was already starting to slip closer towards the horizon. It probably would have made more sense to leave in the morning, but no one wanted to stay.

Katerina laughed softly, tying back her long hair. "Plenty of time for that later. For now...we can let your uncle do the heavy lifting."

The uncle in question heard them speaking across the roof and gave his niece a little wink. Evie flashed a grin before turning back to her mother, appraising her with a speculative frown.

"Why aren't you doing it?"

Katerina looked out towards the skyline, lifting her shoulders in a shrug. "It's been a few years."

Years?!

Evie's mouth fell open in surprise.

She's just assumed each of the legendary monarchs had been keeping up their skills, but she should have guessed when Aidan buried their weapons at the base of the mountain. She suddenly wondered how long it had been since her father had shifted into a wolf.

Never one to filter her questions she was about to ask outright, when the sound of a different kind of conversation caught her attention.

Ellanden and Cassiel were standing at the entrance to the roof, as far from the rest of the group as was physically possible, heads bowed together as they spoke back and forth. Most of it was in Fae, too fast for the princess to properly eavesdrop. But whatever was being said, it had a powerful grip on both men. They paused at the same time, staring at each other with the same expression, then came suddenly together in an equally powerful embrace.

Tanya watched them from across the roof, eyes shining, then flashed a quick glance at Katerina before continuing to stash illegal bottles of whiskey into her bag.

Now what was THAT all about?

"All right," Dylan declared, looking every bit the ranger with his cloak and a sword strapped to his belt, "it's time."

The others clustered at a safe distance while Kailas wandered off by himself. Last to join were the fae—who seemed to have tuned back in just in time to remember they hated to fly.

"Each time I swear to myself it will never happen again," Cassiel muttered, watching as the prince vanished in a ball of writhing flames. "And then I find myself here. Time after time."

Evie glanced up at him shyly before slipping her hand into his. "You can sit by me."

He glanced down in surprise, then his face melted into a tender smile. A quick kiss to her forehead then the two of them sprang lightly onto the dragon's wing, settling in for the ride.

The supplies were quickly loaded. The dragon took to the sky. At the last moment, Evie glanced down to see they'd accidently left a candle burning in the window. It didn't matter.

None of them would ever come back to this place again.

Chapter 8

The band of travelers made it a long way before the sun finally kissed the horizon, sending jagged streaks of gold and crimson shooting across the sky. It was quite a distance from their remote mountain retreat, and they probably should have switched dragons at some point, but Katerina was more nervous than she was letting on and her brother was more than happy to oblige.

Evie had overheard the conversation before they left, hiding outside the kitchen.

"What if they hate me?" the queen had murmured, head bowed to her chest.

Kailas' eyes tightened and he shook his head. "They won't."

"But what if they do—"

"They *won't*," he'd insisted, tilting his head to coax a smile. "They didn't hate me, did they?"

There was a pause.

"A lot of them did, Kailas."

The twins laughed quietly, then stood in silence—minds blurring over the last few years.

They had each lost a child, and recovered them. Lost a mother, and recovered her. Lost a crown, *twice*...but there was still a chance they could recover that, too. Many times, they'd stood in that same spot—arguing, consoling, weeping. It was in that exact place Katerina had asked him to take the throne.

"I don't know if I ever thanked you," she murmured, "for stepping in the way you did."

He flashed a tender smile, sweeping back her hair.

"You gave me ten years, Katy. The least I could do is give you ten years in return."

Maybe Ellanden has a point. Maybe I do tend to spy.

The princess snapped back to the present to find herself still sandwiched between her mother and the fae. Cassiel had yet to open his eyes since their departure, his jaw was clenched impossibly tight. And there was a chance he was praying, while her mother was lost in thought.

She peered up at her quietly, trying to think of something helpful. Her father pushed restlessly to his feet and paced along the dragon's back, staring in the direction of his homeland.

"So you're Belarian...but you've never been to the capital?"

It was the first time anyone had spoken in a long while and it took a moment to respond. Seth glanced up in surprise, then bowed his head quickly. No matter how many days they'd spent together at the villa, the shifter was still a little overwhelmed to be speaking directly to his king.

"No, Sire." He blushed the moment he said it. Since the day they met, Dylan had been trying to banish the title from his vocabulary—with very little success. "I come from a small village. Very few people in my pack have ever travelled to the capital city."

Dylan nodded thoughtfully, walking to the very tip of Kailas' wing. He might have ruled a land that spanned a thousand leagues, but the man knew every inch of his kingdom. Even now, he was trying to place the tiny hamlet. It was next to the Tyburn River, not far from an old fort...

"I heard a funny story about your village," he murmured, glancing over the side to the trees streaking past below. "It seems you have a quaint tradition—throwing yourselves off a cliff."

His gaze lifted, locking on to the shifter's face.

"It seems you were kind enough to share this tradition...with my daughter."

Seth froze perfectly still, looking like he was about to throw up. Dylan let him stay like that for a good long while before his lips pulled back in a terrifying smile.

"That village of yours...show me where it is."

He gestured him forward, to the edge of the dizzying thousand-foot drop.

"Leave the boy alone," Cassiel ordered, never opening his eyes. "You know Everly. She probably tripped over that cliff all by herself."

It would have stung less if it wasn't partially true.

The princess jutted up her chin before pressing the tips of her fingers into the dragon's charcoal scales. "You know what, Uncle? I think it's time for a little show."

Kailas was more than happy to oblige.

Less than a second later, that peaceful sunset vanished into a chorus of screams as the dragon pointed his noise downward and shot straight as an arrow back to the earth.

"Honey—stop!"

"No, no, no!"

"Are you crazy?!"

"Kailas Alexander—I will KILL you in your sleep!"

They evened out so suddenly, it was as if they were never dropping at all. Most of the friends started laughing once they'd retained their equilibrium, but the Lord of the Fae was incensed.

"Before sundown tonight—"

"Leave the boy alone," Dylan quoted with a grin. He was the only one who never minded such antics. Quite the contrary, they thrilled him beyond words. "He's just having a bit of fun."

Evie smoothed her hair with a breathless smile, smacking at Seth's arm. "Just like your fairytales?"

He gave her a hard look, hands clenched white upon the dragon. "You are all...without question...certifiably insane."

⁂

NEEDLESS TO SAY, TENSIONS were running a bit high by the time they decided to make camp.

The second the dragon landed, Cassiel picked up the prince's clothes and stalked angrily into the forest. As if that wasn't enough, the flicker of a vengeful fire was soon to follow.

"Cass..." Kailas called with a hint of desperation, shielding himself from sight. "There are logistics here...yes, I know you're angry...my *daughter* is ten paces away..."

The princess glanced after them with a grin before turning to her mother. While the rest of them broke into old habits—checking the perimeter, gathering firewood, pitching the tents, locating the whiskey—the queen was standing on her own, looking uncharacteristically uncertain.

When she saw Evie watching, she flashed a tight smile.

"Your father spent most nights as a wolf," she murmured, "running midnight trails through the mountains. Cassiel travelled often with Tanya, less near the end. Aiden left to hunt..."

Evie softened with a heartbreaking expression.

"But never you?"

Her mother shook her head.

For five years, she hadn't taken a single step outside that villa. Five years with nothing left to comfort her but the whisper of birds and the scent of her daughter's perfume.

"Just take it one step at a time," Evie murmured gently, taking her hand. "We can help pitch the tents. Then I can find us some—"

"Honey?"

That flash of uncertainty vanished into a radiant smile.

"...this is *wonderful*."

Oh. Right.

That was the last time the princess worried about her mother.

Considering some of the places the children had slept not long before, the camp was nothing short of extravagant. A tight circle of tents orbited a roaring fire, each stocked with enough weapons and supplies to attempt a small siege. There was enough food to last a week without having to replenish, but though they were only a day's journey from Belaria they still felt the need to hunt.

...they felt the need to use those weapons.

"I'll do it," Ellanden volunteered quickly, not seeing the way his father froze the second he reached for a bow. "Ash can come with me. There's a glen a few miles south, I saw it when we were flying over. We'll be back before you—"

"Not tonight."

Unlike the young fae, Dylan's eyes didn't miss a thing. They rested only a moment upon his stricken friend before turning with a twinkling smile to the other wolf standing amongst them.

"This one's never been so deep inside Belaria." He cocked his head invitingly towards the trees. "What kind of sovereign would I be if I didn't offer a tour?"

It was a gracious save, one that was all but lost on the younger generation. Cassiel offered a fleeting look of gratitude before drifting towards the fire.

Ellanden was disappointed, but Seth lit up with a boyish smile.

"Really?" he asked a little breathlessly. "You want me to come with you?"

Dylan inclined his head with the trace of a grin.

"If you stop calling me 'Sire'. On that note..." He slipped off his cloak and boots, preparing to make the transformation. "Probably best if you don't speak at all."

A collective flinch rippled through the rest of them. You'd be hard-pressed to find a more talented hunter, but the wolves of Belaria weren't exactly known for the cleanest of kills. The last time Dylan tracked down dinner as a wolf, Tanya swore she found a claw in the middle of hers.

It was enough to spark a small mutiny, but the young shifter was in such heaven no one said a word. They simply lifted their hands as the air shimmered and two wolves bounded into the trees.

"Contingency plan," Tanya muttered. "I'll make some stew."

If possible, this was met with an even worse reaction, but the princess had no intention of sticking around to see it. Ellanden had yet to set down his bow, and if his attention wasn't diverted quickly he'd soon be setting off with the vampire all the same—a vague competition in mind.

"How about you and I get some water?" she suggested quickly, yanking on the edge of his sleeve. The bow came down, paired with an incredulous look. "The river's just down there."

The fae followed her gaze, while his father exhaled in silent relief.

"Well that sounds exhilarating, Everly. Thank you for thinking of me."

"Come on," she muttered with a roll of her eyes, steering him towards the ravine. "I'll attack you halfway there, then you can use your sword."

THE PRINCESS AND THE fae walked along in silence as the moon rose slowly above the trees. It was a very old forest, the kind that probably used to be governed by the Fae themselves, but had been lost over time to the hands of men. Sounds were softer, nothing crackled or snapped. The trees whispered instead, bending towards the young companions with the weight of a thousand secrets.

"Are you wearing perfume?"

Evie's head snapped up as the prince glanced simultaneously down at her. For a few silent seconds, she simply blinked in surprise. Then she remembered the bottle in her room.

"No," she said quickly. "I mean—yes. Some must have gotten on my hands."

He took her wrist without thinking, holding it to his face.

"Jasmine and...wisteria?"

"Freesia."

"I think you're wrong."

"I'm not."

They walked a while longer, listening to the sound of the river as it weaved slowly through the ancient trees. Both were carrying empty flasks, bumping quietly against their legs.

After a few more minutes, she glanced up at him again.

"When we first arrived, you asked for your father." She hesitated a moment, feeling almost shy. "I know you were just as desperate to see your mother...why did you ask for only him?"

He was quiet for a while before answering. "My mother could survive the death of a child. My father never could."

This struck her as an incredibly strange thing to say. Her aunt loved as passionately and deeply as anyone she knew. And to suggest that anything could defeat his father?

It must have shown on her face, because the fae smiled faintly.

"My father was born immortal. He grew up with the concept of eternity. The loss of something can never be so great as when you had the chance to keep it forever." His voice hitched ever so slightly. "My mother is mortal. She wouldn't have to live with such a thing for long."

The princess frowned deeply, staring at the silvery trail. They had almost reached the water—a few more minutes and they'd be sloshing back up the hill. She walked alongside him a split second longer, torn with silent indecision, then threw out a sudden hand to catch his sleeve.

"Landi, I have to tell you—"

"I already know," he said softly. "My mother told me when I arrived."

Both of them paused in the middle of the trail. A literal ache throbbed in her chest as she stared up at him, while he was gazing with a peculiar expression into the forest.

"Your mother—"

"She's the reason he came back," he interrupted, still staring into the trees. "I doubt Aidan could have made him return otherwise."

The princess dropped her eyes, at a complete loss. "You never told me there was such a place."

He stared a moment longer, then forced himself back to the present. "Because I wish there wasn't."

She shook her head slowly, resisting every urge to take his hand. There was already a crispness to his words. In such times, he never responded well to physical comforts.

"And your mother?" she asked. "How did she...?"

He opened his mouth to answer then turned away suddenly, shaking his head.

They continued down to the river.

It didn't take long to fill the flasks. There were only four; the rest had been surrendered to the communal liquor stash and couldn't be used. They capped them carefully, stepping back out of the water, when Ellanden turned to her suddenly, a reflection of starlight dancing in his eyes.

"It's why you asked me to come with you."

Her boot slipped in the mud, almost toppling her right there.

"No, I...I needed help with the..."

She lifted the flasks helplessly, dropping them back against her leg. It was impossible to lie to a fae. Better not to even try. But such logic had never stopped her before.

"You know I probably would have spilled these on my own."

He stared at her a moment, then leaned down suddenly and kissed her cheek. "Thank you."

She looked up at him in surprise. "...you're welcome."

They shared a fleeting smile, then continued walking up the mountain.

IT WASN'T A LONG JOURNEY back to the camp. The friends could hear the sounds of it almost as soon as they left the river. But the night had taken an unexpectedly serious turn, and they were both determined to lighten their spirits before rejoining the others.

They took their time, telling jokes and sharing stories. Letting themselves relax back into an old dynamic that felt lifetimes in the past. A time when responsibilities had been tasked to the older generation. When they were still children whose days were filled with whimsy and laughter.

No dark prophecies to command them. No secret adversaries prowling in the shadows.

For a brief moment they allowed themselves to believe it was just another family camping trip, same as a thousand times before. When the years felt younger, when the woods felt safe.

That's when they heard the screaming.

The attack came so suddenly, there was almost no way to prepare for it. One second, all was peaceful in the ancient forest. A second later, a horde of painted warriors flooded out of the trees.

Evie and Ellanden froze in the middle of the trail, staring in horror.

They were slightly taller than your average person, built like oxen, with stout blades gripped in both hands. The attack had been carefully timed and coordinated, clearly counting on the element of surprise, and while they hadn't seen the pair yet the rest of their camp had been overrun.

Tents were capsized and flattened under a swarm of pounding feet, pitching forward and tumbling with terrible accuracy into the fire. The stacks of provisions Kailas had flown so carefully over the mountains were swiftly plundered as well—some destroyed in the chaotic scramble, while others were snatched up with equal speed and reclaimed as a stolen prize. Those chilling screams echoed with every passing second, designed to disorient and craze. But while such tactics might have worked for them in the past, the painted bandits had clearly underestimated their opponents.

There had been a single moment of surprise. A moment when those gathered around the camp had raised their heads in unison, staring with wide eyes at the mayhem headed their way.

Then the surprise passed…and they started reaching for weapons.

In a fraction of a second, the momentum shifted—flying straight back at the invaders as the little clearing ripped apart at the seams. Asher and Aidan leapt to their feet at the same time, fangs bared, hands at the ready. They stood together for only a moment before flying straight into the enemy forces, vanishing like wisps of deadly smoke. It was possible to track them only by the screams that followed, by the trail of mangled bodies that followed in their wake.

Kailas picked up a sword, slicing neatly into the belly of a man who'd leapt towards him, while his dainty daughter somersaulted quickly past another, severing his legs with a single swing of an axe. Serafina had been slightly distracted when the warriors arrived, still trying to coax her sister-in-law away from the idea of cooking, and had abandoned the idea of conventional weapons altogether, fracturing one man with a ladle before bludgeoning another with a copper plate.

Freya was the only one to let out a shriek—she did so only because one of the flaming tents had caught the hem of her borrowed dress on fire. She glanced down for just a moment, watching as the shimmering fabric dissolved into ash. Then she tore off the offending portion and charged right into the center of the horde with a vengeful cry—waves of liquid light rippling over her skin.

Tanya was perched halfway up a tree, hurling tiny daggers with deadly accuracy. Cassiel picked an arrow from a stray quiver, twirling it once through his fingers before plunging it straight through a painted face. The result was barbaric enough to send five others scattering away.

Who needs a bow when you've got arrows?

A valid question, one those painted warriors were asking themselves. But Katerina Damaris had never been content to play with blades and arrows. The queen had bigger tricks up her sleeve.

"Get down!"

Her friends didn't need to be told twice.

There was a sound like a typhoon as a wave of dragon fire swept into the clearing—followed immediately by a chorus of hysterical screams. Those screams fell abruptly silent a moment later, leaving a chilled silence in their wake—one contrasted sharply by the blistering heat that followed.

It felt like a lifetime, but only a few seconds had passed. The bandits were dazed but rallying. Evie and Ellanden glanced at each other as the flasks went splashing to their feet.

"Looks like you'll get to use that sword after all."

They took off without another word, charging into the heart of the battle with matching fearsome cries. Asher materialized beside them a second later, and they worked in tandem. The princess shot out bursts of fire while the vampire guarded her back. The fae stood with a few paces behind them with a bow, felling each of their fiery victims before they could set the forest ablaze.

Cosette abandoned her axe and joined them, grabbing a bow for herself. Freya had to be forcibly extracted—perched on the back of a brutish swordsman, firing light into his skull.

"Would you stop playing and get down here?" the fae chided, firing off a trio of arrows as she slid across the clearing. "There's work to be done."

The witch hopped down a second later, beaming and smeared with blood.

"...what happened to my dress?"

A distant howl echoed through the trees, growing steadily closer. The friends glanced up in anticipation, while their painted attackers whirled around to see which direction it was coming from, wondering what other nightmares could possibly have been lurking in the ancient trees.

They didn't have to wait long to find out.

No sooner had Evie heard the call of her father than he burst onto the scene, landing with a blistering snarl in the center of the clearing, another darker wolf shadowing by his side.

He took a single look around the clearing, sky blue eyes assessing the safety of everyone he loved in a sweeping glance. Then he threw back his head with a blood-curdling roar.

At this point, the bandits seemed to have realized they'd made a mistake. They'd seen only the blaze of a campfire and had never imagined the people that might be sitting alongside. It was a fool who'd pick a fight with a vampire or a fae. The arrival of the wolves seemed like a nightmare.

The three women shooting fire were a trauma to be processed at a later date.

The only thing they had working for them was the numbers, and they had those in spades. It was enough to keep them going. Enough to keep them thinking they might actually have a chance.

But then something strange happened...*another* howl echoed through the trees.

At this point their enemies scattered, while the friends looked up in surprise.

Bows tightened and blades glinted in the moonlight as they clustered closer together, spinning around just as the bandits had done to see from which direction the new danger might arrive. Cassiel unsheathed a breathtaking silver sword, standing in front of Ellanden, while Katerina lifted both hands slowly, eyes darting from tree to tree. An unnatural stillness had fallen over the vampires, the witch was wedged between the others, and a snarling wolf stood tall at Cosette's side.

For whatever reason Dylan shifted on the spot, pulling on his cloak with one hand and grabbing his daughter with another—ready to rip apart this new danger with his bare hands.

But the king was unprepared for what came out of those trees.

There was a rustling of ferns, a whisper of movement, then a dozen massive wolves melted out of the shadows, eyes bright and gleaming, a silver-tipped behemoth leading the way.

Dylan straightened up slowly, trying to catch his breath.

"...Atticus?"

In a flash, the wolf vanished. A familiar face sprang up in its place.

"Impeccable timing, Your Majesty." The aged councilman sank into a reverent bow as the wolves behind him bent their knees. "And let me be first to say...welcome home."

Chapter 9

The return of the Belarian king could be overshadowed by only one thing: the resurrection of his missing daughter.

Evie had no idea how the news had spread so quickly. There had been no scouts, every member of Atticus' hunting party had escorted them all the way back to the city gates. But by the time they arrived at the capital, it seemed as though the entire kingdom was waiting for them.

The second she stepped onto the cobbled streets a deafening chorus of applause rose up to greet her, echoing louder from every direction and stealing the breath straight out of her chest.

She startled reflexively, clinging to her father for balance. Both vampires discreetly flinched at the same time, raising a hand to their over-sensitized ears.

"Is this for you?" she gasped, eyes widening in astonishment as what looked like every citizen of Belaria poured onto the streets. "Did they come here for you?"

Dylan shook his head with a little smile. "Listen to what they're saying."

PRINCESS! PRINCESS! PRINCESS!

The chant thundered from the very heart of the city, blending into a single wall of sound. As they proceeded down the street she heard it from a thousand screaming voices, from a thousand beaming faces—each one rejoicing in wild celebration as their missing princess returned home.

Windows were thrown open, flags and banners waved frantically in the air. A pack of children raced in front of them, shrieking with laughter while a shower of ivory petals rained down upon the streets. More people fell into step behind them, lifting their voices in jubilant cries.

By the time they reached the palace, the sound had swelled to such deafening heights the princess was no longer able to hear. Her ears were throbbing and a stream of blinding tears poured from her eyes.

She paused at the top of the steps, turning around to face them. Never would she forget the sight of it. Never could she have imagined such an overwhelming display of love.

Her body trembled under the weight of it. That rhythmic chant rose up through the marble, tickling the bottoms of her feet. She wanted to say something, but couldn't find the breath.

In the end, she simply lifted her hand.

The crowds erupted in response, soaring to new levels as the palace doors opened and they were beckoned inside. She stood there a moment longer, still waving, tears streaming freely down her cheeks. Then the world spun dizzily and she reached for her father.

He caught her just as both legs gave out, carrying her inside.

<hr />

THE SECOND THE DOORS swung shut, the sound abruptly vanished—leaving a ringing silence in its wake. The friends took a moment to recover, trembling slightly as the echoes faded away.

"Is it always like that when you leave the palace?" Freya asked incredulously, pressing her fingers to the wall as she struggled to find her balance.

Evie glanced back towards the doors, heart pounding in her chest. "Yeah...every time."

She unwrapped her arms slowly from her father's neck, lowering her feet to the floor.

The rest of them were looking just as unsteady.

Asher was cringing at the edge of the group with Seth, a hand still raised to his ears. Cosette was gripping the edge of her mother's dress, like a child afraid of being lost in the crowd.

Ellanden was staring in silence towards the doors, no doubt wondering if he'd receive a similar greeting upon his return to the Ivory City. His expression was difficult to read, but strangely enough the princess was willing bet he was hoping for something a little more subdued.

There was a weight that came with all that applause, a tangible pressure that grew heavier with each pair of sparkling eyes. It left one feeling loved…and shaken.

There was no avoiding that second part.

"Your Majesties!"

Evie lifted her eyes as a flock of people rushed towards them, surprised to have even heard them over the painful ringing in her ears. Her heart lifted at the sight of so many familiar faces, but it quickened nervously at the same time. The streets of Belaria might have been utter chaos, but the real circus would be the one that happened inside. In the gilded halls of the royal court.

The king had returned. The princess was alive…bringing yet another fateful prophecy to their doorstep. She pulled in a deep breath as they approached, suddenly longing for the woods.

"I don't know if I can do this…"

Dylan glanced down quickly, wrapping an arm around her shoulders. "Don't worry about a thing," he soothed. "Just leave everything to me."

A swarm of nobles rushed towards them, their footsteps echoing on the marble floors. He watched them coming with the same guarded expression as when they'd been attacked in the woods, then pulled Atticus discreetly closer, whispering into the councilman's ear.

"I don't know if I can do this…"

The man smiled ever so slightly before lifting his hands.

"Peace, friends," he called, stopping the onslaught in its tracks. "His Majesty and the royal family are exhausted, having travelled many miles to come home. I promise we will convene to discuss everything in the morning, but for now I implore you to keep your distance and let them rest."

His eyes flickered briefly over the group, lingering on the fire-haired princess.

"I expect they have quite a story to tell..."

THE COURT OF BELARIA would never go directly against the command of their highest council, but neither could they allow their beloved king to merely slip away to his chambers.

They compromised by following him at what was deemed a respectful distance.

"The best of all wishes, my lord!"

"It is an answer to our prayers!"

Dylan raised his hand with a tight smile as he and the others swept down the great hall in a single group—keeping in constant motion lest they be swarmed the moment they stopped. His wife was a bit more gracious, calling back several replies, while the children clustered safely in the middle.

What must they be thinking? Evie thought, peering past her boyfriend's shoulder at the crowds of people lining the hall. *Do they assume we were kidnapped? That we ran away?*

Asher stumbled suddenly and she caught his arm.

"Are you okay?"

He nodded painfully, finding his balance. "I think that welcome party broke my ears..."

Aidan slowed his pace immediately, taking her place at the vampire's side, while she fell back towards the edge of the group—drifting alongside Seth as they continued their hasty escape.

Unlike the others, the shifter was having trouble ignoring the curious stares of the lords and ladies clustered around them. Neither could he tune out the whispers that followed every step.

There was no question as to the young man's humble origins, since his hair was braided in the style of the packs that roamed the western mountains. Yet he was walking a step behind the king.

The concept of whispering was a bit passive-aggressive in the land of shifters to begin with, and it didn't help that he'd been asking himself the same questions since they'd arrived. By the time they reached the heavy doors at the end of the corridor he paused uncertainly, hesitant to go inside.

"I should wait out here," he murmured, shifting uneasily as the great commanders of Belaria studied him from afar. "Or stay at one of the local taverns until your business is done."

Evie turned to him in surprise. "Don't be ridiculous—"

"I'm serious, Everly. Give me some of our coin." He took a quick step back when those curious eyes widened at his proximity. "I shouldn't even be talking to you. I shouldn't be here."

Seven hells!

While the others bade an awkward farewell to the people tracking them, trying to slip away into their chambers, she pulled him onto an adjoining balcony, away from prying eyes.

"What the hell are you talking about?" she demanded. "You shouldn't *be* here??"

He clenched his jaw, staring out towards the sky.

"I was born in a hovel. I spent time as a slave."

She tilted her head curiously, waiting for the punchline, then caught herself just as he looked back over, making a concerted effort to clear her face.

"None of that matters. Can't you see that?" She threw her arms in a wide gesture. "This is just a building, Seth. And those are just people. Look at what we've *done*."

"Just a building," he muttered, eyes sweeping the carved stone.

She stepped right in front of him, refusing to be dissuaded. "Yes—just a building. Anything past that is all inside your head. You belong here, same as the rest of us."

His gaze rose slowly to a framed portrait above her head.

Oh...right.

She grabbed his arm quickly, angling him the other way.

"Were you holding a mink?"

"I've always hated that painting," she muttered, pulling in another deep breath. "You've been with us from the beginning. You're one of us. You don't see Freya acting like this."

They both glanced over to where the witch in question was edging covertly towards one of the guards stationed outside the doorway, no doubt intending to 'surprise' him into shifting.

Ellanden caught her arm without breaking conversation, pulling her back to his side.

"I came along to protect Cosette," Seth said quietly, eyes flickering to the lovely fae. She had doubled back to wait for the rest of them and was standing in the middle of the hallway, surrounded by a host of guards. "...I'd say that's taken care of."

"And what of the stone?" Evie said sharply. "What of the prophecy?"

"I was not given your prophecy—"

"But you believe in it," she pressed. "You believe in what we're doing."

He threw up his hands, glancing desperately around the palace. "Of course I do, but...does it matter? So will everyone here. There are protocols to this sort of thing. Places of privilege, levels of rank. I cannot be standing in the same hallway as my king."

She looked him over fondly, softening with a faint smile.

"'Does it matter,'" she quoted before shaking her head. "It happens to matter a great deal."

They stared at each other a second longer, then she linked her arm deliberately through his and escorted him back into the palace. He followed along robotically, more surprised than anything else. Then he froze perfectly still as she paused in front of everyone, squeezing his hand.

"Your chambers are next to mine."

THE CHILDREN MIGHT all have been royalty, but the palaces in which they resided were quite different. The Belarian palace was a fortress against incursions and cold weather—scorching in the summertime, then bracing for winter snow. The castle in the High Kingdom was taken straight out of a children's storybook. High turrets, cranking drawbridge, balmy forests that bordered on every side. Taviel was the most enchanting of them all—a city of pure ivory, set on the crest of three waterfalls, deep in a starlit forest, hidden in the middle of a dazzling sea.

Different designs for different kingdoms, but one tenet remained the same. If royalty was to be present, it would be cloistered. Set apart at a distance, to mingle only as it wished.

The result was a residence *inside* a residence, forbidden even to servants and equipped with everything the friends might need. Their chambers were lavish and adjoined, but separated from the rest of the palace—set in a small circle with a shared dining area and living space in between.

To the rest of the world, it was a place of constant speculation.

To the princess, it was merely home.

"Good *morning*!"

She wandered into the dining room with a broad smile, feeling quite literally as though it was the first time in ten years she'd gotten to sleep in her own bed. To say that she'd reveled in the luxury was underselling it. She'd spent two hours soaking in a tub, then slept until mid-afternoon.

"Morning?" Cosette teased, looking a great deal more put together than she'd been the previous night. "I think we passed morning quite some time ago."

Evie dismissed this in a grand gesture and grabbed an empty plate.

The servants might have been banned from the residence, but when it was known the royal family was dining privately, as opposed to joining the rest of the court in the grand dining hall, the chef prepared dishes to be sent up and eaten there instead. These were usually retrieved by whoever happened to wake up first, and were dumped without ceremony in the center of the table.

"Aw," she grinned, examining the various platters, "they made such effort for you."

The fae princess rolled her eyes, sipping daintily from a cup of cider.

As the palaces of five kingdoms varied greatly, their cuisine differed as well. For the Belarians, this meant heartier fare in the cooler seasons, with a summer of cheeses and bread. The High Kingdom claimed to have some cultural specialties of their own—though it usually consisted of whatever happened to be found in the nearby forest—and the Fae were somewhat of a mystery.

The concept of vegetarianism didn't play well amongst the shifters. Each time someone tried to explain, their faces collectively blanked, as if they honestly didn't understand. Eventually, they had compromised by deciding the fair folk subsisted generally on nectar and prayers. Having neither in great supply, whenever a delegation was visiting they were plied with copious amounts of fruit.

True to form, almost half the table was laden with samples from the various orchards that surrounded the city walls. There were platters of peaches and berries, plums and pears, all arranged in what hoped to be an aesthetically pleasing design. Some had been drenched in honey. These had already begun to capsize, melting into a sticky puddle between the pastries and milk.

"It's like they think we're hummingbirds," Cosette murmured, perched on the windowsill with her glass. "Or maybe some kind of bat."

Evie looked up with a sudden smile. "Speak of the devil..."

Asher flashed a sarcastic grin as he breezed out of the hallway, coming up behind her chair to kiss the side of her neck. "You know, I've never understood that comparison."

"Heard that, did you? Your ears must be working." She lifted her eyes mischievously, then reached out in surprise when he handed her a mug of jasmine tea. "Did the chef bring this up?"

He shook his head casually, sinking into the chair beside her own. "I made it."

She took a steaming sip, beaming over the side of the glass.

Disgusting...and incredibly sweet.

A door opened at the other end of the residence, and a few seconds later Ellanden shuffled sleepily down the hall. The handsome fae was looking far less composed than usual, with bare feet and tousled hair. His braids were missing. He had also somehow forgotten his shirt.

"Morning," he yawned, settling into the nearest chair and poking the honey-soaked peaches with a little grin. "Oh good...mulch."

Evie snorted, but felt the need to defend.

"Leave them alone. At least they're trying."

The fae kicked back in his chair, bypassing the fruit altogether and buttering a slice of bread. "You know, Leonor refuses to come here anymore. He thinks the court is either trying to mock him, or simply starve him to death."

The princess snorted again, picturing the stoic councilman. "This is Belaria. No reason we can't do both."

The others laughed quietly, while Asher surveyed the fae with a wicked grin.

"You look tired, Landi. Didn't get much sleep?"

As if to answer his question Freya drifted down the same hallway, wearing the prince's missing tunic like a dress. Cosette gagged into her cider while the fae pushed immediately to his feet, giving the witch a leisurely kiss before pulling her down onto his lap.

Looks like she found a way out of that gown after all...

The friends had been too astonished by the sudden arrival of the wolves to process much of anything else happening in the forest that night. Pieces of the painted bandits were still littering the campsite, and most everything they'd brought with them was now a pile of ashes.

But the princess remembered quite clearly the look on Cassiel and Tanya's faces when their son had dropped his bow and lifted the lovely witch straight off the ground for a passionate kiss.

They had been...surprised, to say the least.

It hadn't helped that she was still flickering with waves of magic, or that her stolen dress had been singed away up to the thigh, leaving her bare legs wrapped around his waist.

"No, not much sleep." The prince flashed a wicked grin in return, spearing a candied apple for himself. "But you, Ash? You look very well-rested."

The vampire opened his mouth with a cutting reply, but in a bout of fortunate timing their final member appeared at the end of the hall.

"Good morning," Seth greeted them with a bright smile, one that faded ever so slightly when he saw the life-size portrait on the wall beside him. Aldrich Hale was a hard man. They'd attempted to soften him by placing a pair of doves in his arms...to a slightly bizarre effect.

"Admiring the portraits," Ellanden teased. "Don't worry, peasant. We'll commission one for you as well. You'll be dressed in the finest armor. Cradling a mouse."

"I always figured it was a before and after kind of thing," Freya murmured, stealing the fae's toast. "Here's the princess holding a bunny. Here's the bunny after the princess shifted and—"

"Let's keep this civilized, shall we?" Evie interrupted lightly, gesturing to the table. "As you can see, we're featuring some delightful vegetarian cuisine..."

For the next half-hour the friends feasted to their hearts' content, forgetting the troubles that had driven them to the palace and enjoying the fact that they were simply there. Despite their best efforts there had always been a layer of tension at the villa, but for the first time in longer than they cared to admit they were looking at the path that lay before them with a tiny spark of hope.

They had an army behind them. They had a kingdom behind that. They had a trio of fire-breathing dragons and were building enough momentum to shift the tide.

Maybe there's a chance we can do this after all...

"So how does this work?" Seth finally asked when they finished, gesturing to the portrait as he leaned back in his chair. "Does everyone here get a painting? And is everyone required to share that painting with their spirit animal...because mine's going to take a bit of work."

He glanced significantly at Asher, who simply shook his head.

"I'm just assuming it's a vole."

"The fae aren't into paintings," Evie answered seriously. "But if they *really* like you, they might give you a giant bird."

Ellanden chuckled under his breath, having been bitten by said bird before.

"Seriously." Seth straightened up, glancing about curiously for the first time. "How does this work with your families mixing bloodlines? How can some of you be heir to multiple thrones?"

There was a pause, during which they tried not to groan.

Since they were just children, the councils of no fewer than four different kingdoms had been asking the same question. Their answers tended to be both territorial and vague.

Far too territorial for the children's taste.

"It's complicated," Cosette finally answered.

Seth prompted her with a little smile. "Let's make it easier...what's your full name?"

Not much easier.

She considered a moment, then extended her hand. "Cosette Damaris of House Elénarin."

Seth repeated it back, eyes tightening in confusion. "My father's name," she explained, "my mother's house."

The shifter nodded slowly, trying to keep it straight.

"So...what about Ellanden?"

"He's just Ellanden," she answered simply. "Most fae don't have last names, just a house."

"But won't people mix them up?" Freya chimed in curiously.

Ellanden rested his chin on her shoulder, giving her a tight squeeze. "Relatively speaking, there aren't that many fae left," he answered. "We're talking thousands, not tens of thousands."

"Why?"

"Fae make people want to kill them," Asher said lightly.

Ellanden flashed him a hard look. "More like countless instances of genocide perpetuated in large part by the Damaris—"

"My *name*," Cosette interjected swiftly, "not my *house*." The rest turned to her incredulously, and she shrugged. "I always figured that exempted me from most of the blame."

"So what about you?" Freya turned to the shifter when the laughter died down. "My mistress never told me, I'm assuming she didn't want me tracking down my family. What's your full name?"

Seth blushed, dropping his eyes to the ground.

"I don't...uh...I don't have one."

The others stared at him blankly.

"Where I come from, most people don't." He took a slender knife from the table, spinning it absentmindedly in his hands. "Packs show allegiance in other ways—kind of like houses, I guess—but individual surnames never really happen."

"Then how do you differentiate between yourselves?" Ellanden asked in surprise. "There are so many of you...like rabbits."

"We live in isolated villages," Seth replied briskly, tossing the knife on the table. "I've never met anyone else with my name."

"So what name would you two share?" Freya blurted without speaking, eyes drifting between the shifter and the fae. "I mean, if you ever..."

She seemed to realize what she was saying and stopped herself quickly.

Not that it mattered. The damage was already done. An awkward silence fell over the table, and the fae's cheeks burned red as a flame.

"I don't know," Seth finally answered, flashing a tight smile. "We wouldn't, I guess."

Cosette stared out the window in silence.

"Maybe you could join her house?" Evie suggested hopefully, anything to get them past the sudden tension. "It's happened. *Super* rarely. But there have been times when a fae lets someone out of the bloodline into their house. Just look at my Uncle Kailas."

"Yeah, but he was the only person in, like, a thousand years," Ellanden answered without thinking, not seeing the collective flinch. "Plus, my father always said it was a bad idea."

The princess glared daggers, while Asher kicked him under the table.

"So why aren't you at this meeting with the rest of them?" Seth replied coolly. Unlike the others, he was the only one to have gotten fully dressed, not realizing their parents would have already departed for the High Chamber. "Or did someone forget to invite you?"

A tense silence fell over the table, then dissipated just as quickly.

"These meetings do not yet involve the prophecy," Evie deflected as the others became suddenly absorbed with their food. "They're only in regards to the crown. That has always been for our parents to settle. It doesn't yet concern us."

Even as she said them, the words felt stilted and false. It wasn't that they weren't true, perhaps the time for them had simply passed. Seth seemed to be thinking along the same lines.

"Doesn't yet concern you?" he repeated. "It didn't sound that way when we arrived."

PRINCESS! PRINCESS! PRINCESS!

No matter how much time had passed, Evie couldn't get the pounding voices out of her head. A strange feeling of apprehension swept over her, quickening her heartbeat. Then Seth finally took pity on her and changed the subject instead.

"So they're busy and we have a free day." His lips quirked into a little smile, as if the concept of 'free time' was a source of great amusement. "How are we to spend the hours?"

The tension vanished in a heartbeat as the friends shared the same excited look.

"Actually, it's funny you should ask..."

Chapter 10

"I don't believe it," Seth murmured. "You have your own arena."

Only in Belaria could such a thing have been a natural fixture at the palace. While the other kingdoms had training grounds for their troops as well, they were usually built at a distance for the sake of decorum. But fighting was deeply ingrained in the shifter way of life. Whether it was training, teaching, or mere exhibition...the arena and all its glory was only a short walk away.

Despite its grisly function, it was a strangely peaceful location—especially when it was empty of people like it was that day. Nestled in a wide grassy field between the forest and the palace, Evie had spent many happy days watching as the warriors of her kingdom battled each other across the lawn. Many times, the match was hastily paused as she was caught toddling into the middle. Other times, the troops were treated to a fully-fledged tantrum as she demanded to ride a wolf.

"There's some irony for you." Ellanden glanced at the shifter with a devilish grin. "And to think, you'd only just escaped..."

Seth opened his mouth to answer, then grabbed a sword from the rack instead—whipping it through the air in a deadly slice. The fae immediately picked a blade for himself, moving backwards with an anticipatory smile as the two began sparring across the grass.

"That's perfect," Asher murmured, folding his arms. "Now they can finally kill each other."

The princess flashed a grin, watching as they blurred in a dizzying display of acrobatics and steel. But the archery range was waiting just a little ways off, drawing her eyes away from the rest

"You know...we never got to finish our competition." She glanced up at the vampire, tilting her head with a little smile. "From the night of the carnival. They called us for dinner first."

Cosette's eyes shot to them with a peculiar expression—the girl had been hiding behind the targets, but the memory was not nearly so fresh—while Asher's lips curved with a little smile.

"If only you'd listened and sat down with the rest of us," he teased, winding his fingers through hers. "Then maybe we could have avoided this prophecy mess altogether."

She backed away with a grin, tugging him closer. "Best out of three?"

"You really want me to beat you at your own palace?" he quipped, trailing after her. "What if some of those loyal subjects happen to see? I can't imagine how that would devastate morale..."

"How about we put some money on it?" she replied. "Then again, I have the treasury of two kingdoms at my disposal...while you're technically homeless."

It was a bold choice, especially considering some of the places they'd been. But the friends had never played lightly. If anything, the newfound bond between them had upped her game.

"Homeless." His eyebrows rose dangerously as his dark eyes caught the sun. The idea of archery was forgotten as he began stalking her across the grass. "Touché, little princess."

She grinned in spite of herself, feeling the rush of blood to her cheeks as she backed away from him, taking extra care not to trip. There was something inescapably predatory about it, and even though she loved him madly it was impossible not to be just a little bit afraid. Cosette and Freya started openly laughing while the boys battled behind them, oblivious to the glacial chase.

She heard the clash of metal on metal, punctuated with occasional taunts.

"I thought you'd be better than this," Seth teased, ducking as the fae's blade sliced exactly where his neck had been a second before.

"I didn't," Ellanden countered, rolling quickly over the grass to avoid a retaliatory jab to the side. "You are meeting my precise expectations."

Evie angled towards them discreetly, still backing away.

"Let's not do anything hasty," she warned, lifting her hands as the vampire paced towards her. "You remember what happened the last time you attacked me."

He flashed with a bewitching smile. "...you took off all my clothes?"

Yes, I did. Shit.

"It was probably the time before," she clarified hastily, raising her voice to get the fae's attention. "At any rate, I'd hate to *call for reinforcements*."

The men continued their deadly game, crashing across the field.

"They can't hear you," Asher said with mock concern. "No one's coming." His eyes sparkled as his voice lowered to a deadly purr. "This is typically when you should start to beg."

"Ellanden—the vampire's gone wild!"

The fae detached himself long enough to cast a swift glance towards the standoff before lifting his hands in a childish time-out. For a split second, he scowled—as if the princess had been attempting something quite foolish—then turned rather pragmatically back to the shifter.

"I need to handle this. Could you just surrender?"

Seth straightened up slowly, shaking his head with a grin. "That's a forfeit, Highness."

The prince's blood spiked and all thoughts of rescue vanished from his mind. Evie cast a panicked glance over her shoulder, sensing she'd lost him, then looked back to see Asher standing directly in front of her with a deadly smile. At that point, blind instinct took over.

She leapt with a scream atop the fae's back.

"Everly!" he protested, staggering backwards in surprise. "Get off!"

The girls burst out laughing on the sidelines, while she clung in theatrical terror to the sides of his face. Both arms clamped across his forehead, like a panicked monkey seeking higher ground.

"Join forces!" she commanded.

"You're *strangling* me—"

"JOIN FORCES!"

"If we're joining forces, I side with the vampire," Seth said quickly.

Asher's eyes twinkled with a smile. "That's a wise decision."

"We are *not* joining forces," the fae said crossly, throwing the princess from his back. He shook out his disheveled cloak, then lifted his sword. "I was just about to decapitate the—" The vampire and shifter took a sudden step towards him. "Looks like we're joining forces."

There was a vicious shout as the four of them crashed together on the field.

The friends had sparred together countless times as they were growing up, often in that very arena. But the addition of Seth added a new dynamic. One that was a little less predictable, a little more wild. It was a dynamic the friends happened to enjoy very much.

Seven hells!

Freya screamed in delight, watching as Ellanden spun in a dizzying arc towards the shifter, forcing him backwards across the grass. He had taken Seth's choice of allies rather personally.

He'd armed himself with silver out of spite.

The shifter flinched reflexively, grinning as the fae waved the blade teasingly at his face. In all his time fighting in the arena, never had he come across such dangerous opponents. The only difference was that these weren't actually trying to kill him.

They were content to maim him...with a smile.

"Careful now," the prince called, giving the blade another playful twirl. "My cousin would never forgive me if I marked up that face of yours."

That same cousin fired an arrow at his head.

The woodland princess and the witch had decided to enjoy the fight as spectators rather than joining in. One was already halfway through a flask, calling out increasingly ludicrous pieces of encouragement to her boyfriend. The other had decided to appoint herself referee—firing off arrows with deadly precision whenever she decided things had gotten too far.

"Thank you for that concern." Seth tensed as if to leap over his head, spinning at the last moment in a move the others had never seen before and landing a punishing kick in the fae's ribs. "But I'd be more worried about your partner. She seems to have...lost her way."

Ellanden straightened up with a grimace, then turned around to see for himself.

"Oi!" he cried sharply. "This was *your* idea, remember!"

It was an honest mistake.

The princess and the vampire had been fighting just as fiercely as the others, locked in an eternal struggle, arms clasped around each other's backs...then fighting turned to something else.

Evie flushed with guilt, caught in a forbidden kiss.

In an effort to save face, she bit down on Asher's lip—wriggling free in the same instant and darting back to the fae's side. She avoided his withering stare, looking at the shifter instead.

"That was part of a *strategy*," she preempted before he could say anything. A ringing silence fell between them. "How else was I supposed to get close enough to bite him in return?"

Seth snickered in the background as the fae gave her a measured look.

"I will dispatch the vampire myself," he said stiffly. "As soon as I finish with this one."

Good luck.

"Careful, Ellanden," the shifter echoed the same words of concern. "I don't think he'd allow you the same strategy."

Perhaps it was this final jest that triggered such fierce retaliation.

With a dangerous smile, the fae vanished from sight—appearing a moment later from a completely different direction, coming down on the shifter like a dark angel from the sky.

It was a flawless attack for which there was no defense, one that he'd learned from his father. One that would have ended the fight completely...if the vampire hadn't leapt in the way.

"Asher!"

Even the princess had to call him out, giggling as her partner went flying twenty paces across the field. A pair of punishing arrows was soon to follow, lodging threateningly in the vampire's dark hair as he turned to the others with a breathless smile.

"Sorry I'm late," he said brightly, clapping the shifter on the back. "I got a little distracted back there, but thanks to a recent betrayal I'm currently single. *Loads* of time to fight."

The princess giggled again, while Seth nodded a bit shakily—feeling as though he'd escaped a rather enormous amount of pain. "Yeah, that's...that's some good timing."

There was a muffled profanity as the fae picked himself up off the field.

Most people would have been angry. At the very least, most people would have registered the clearly fractured ribcage and called for a brief pause.

But the fae was smiling, albeit painfully, as he trudged back across the arena.

"Nice of you to join us," he called, picking up his fallen sword. "Sorry about the break-up. You have some blood on your face, by the way."

The vampire wiped his torn lip with a rueful grin, while Evie forgot the concept of alliances completely and ducked discreetly behind Seth.

"I take back everything I said about equality and command you to protect me," she whispered loudly. "That was my picture hanging on the wall. I am your liege lord."

He tilted his head, considering. "...the one of you tending a ferret?"

She pulled sharply on his braids, but the others were no longer listening.

They had fallen into old habits and began circling each other, armed with the same brutal weapons, with the same air of casual nonchalance. The fae in particular had a bit of a grudge to bear, lifting an involuntary hand to his injured chest before giving the sword a quick spin.

"I can never remember, does silver work on vampires?"

Asher smiled dangerously in return. "A blade's a blade," he replied. "Could probably do some damage to you as well."

The fae lifted his eyebrows in surprise. "You think so? Show me."

With no further warning they vanished into thin air—reappearing on the other side of the arena, locked in a deadly struggle that sent waves of vibration rippling through the ground.

It was the kind of battle you couldn't look away from... not that you could really see it. Most of the time, the fae and the vampire were moving too quickly to keep track of. Like most immortals, it was better to stop trying and simply follow the trail of damage they left in their wake. A splash of blood, a splintered tree. A chorus of laughter that raised the hair on the back of their friends' necks.

"Seven hells," Seth murmured, staring in quiet astonishment. "Might they actually—"

"—kill each other?" Evie finished casually.

Unlike the shifter and the witch, the two princess were highly accustomed to such things. In a fit of boredom Cosette had already tired of her vigilance with the bow and was playing with one of the arrows, absentmindedly tracing lyrics into the ground.

"Probably not. They've been trying for years, haven't managed it yet."

It was true. The pair had been doing the same thing since they were five years old, chasing each other around their various palaces, attacking with nursery toys and sticks.

Granted, this older version packed a bit more of a punch.

"Ellanden!"

The trio shouted at the same time, watching as the fae spirited up into the trees and came down in a blur of momentum right on top of the vampire's head. Evie felt the impact all the way across the clearing. Asher let out a soft cry and dropped to one knee.

"What?" the fae called back. "Oh—that? He's fine!"

He just lost several childhood memories and the ability to read.

"How many times do I have to say it?" Evie shouted in return, her palms flickering with a dangerous glow. "You are *not* to break him beyond repair!"

"Get up," he muttered, eyeing the flames warily. "You're making them feel sorry for you."

Asher blinked away stars, trying to remember how to breathe.

"Apologies, friend—I had that backwards!" He flashed a charming smile, lifting the vampire to his feet. "I'll be more careful next time!"

But there wasn't going to be a next time. The second Asher was standing, he disappeared once again—using the prince's own balance against him as he came at him from the other side.

Fae were impossibly fast, and practicing against a vampire had only made him better. He dodged the attack through a combination of talent and luck, but just as he was flipping over the vampire dropped his blade entirely and grabbed the fae's ankle—pulling him back down to earth.

At that point, Ellanden was in trouble.

As long as they were fighting, it was anyone's game. The two were the same age, and when it came to immortality age is what mattered. But there was no beating a vampire in strength. The trick was not to get caught in the first place...the way he was now.

"Shit," he cursed breathlessly, slamming into the grass.

The fae twisted and rolled, trying to free himself, but it was nearly impossible to break a vampire's grip. He tried leaping skyward, but Asher simply held him there like a kite that had snagged itself on a particularly menacing rock. At one point he tried attacking his friend directly, but that was never a good strategy, and with a painful cry he tumbled back to the ground.

"Damn you," he panted breathlessly, unable to stop a smile. "This is cheating—"

"This is *winning*," Asher said patiently, giving him a playful shake. Just a flick of his hand but the fae tossed around like a doll, fingers digging grooves into the earth. "I think it's important for you to stay like this for a while, really internalize the lesson, remember the way it feels."

He dodged a kick to the face, *nearly*, resurfacing with a bloody grin. A valiant effort, but his fingers were still locked around the fae's ankle like a tether, never allowing him to escape.

In an act of desperation Ellanden actually reached up to unlace his boot, but Asher lifted his leg higher—tipping him over in an ungainly pile onto his back.

"Don't bother undressing," he teased. "The shifter was right. I have no interest in you."

By now the others were making their way towards them, breathless with laughter. The fae was laughing, too, but there was only so far he could stretch his pride.

"Enough!" he cried in exasperation. "Everly—use your fire!"

But while the princess had no intention of incinerating her boyfriend, she suddenly recalled they were still in a fight. With an evil smile she switched opponents, using a different power instead.

"Focus, princess!"

The fae shouted in frustration as the girl vanished and a coppery wolf appeared in her place, a fearsome predator that launched itself not at the vampire but at the shifter standing by her side.

Seth was still turning when a pair of heavy paws impacted his chest. He was still gasping in surprise when the two of them toppled backwards, somersaulting wildly across the grass.

That's for the ferret crack!

There were few things more intimidating than a giant wolf landing on top of you. Four legs are better than two, and there really isn't a way to stand your ground.

But the shifter wasn't easily intimidated.

Perhaps by portraits, but not by this.

No sooner had they hit the grass than the man disappeared and a snarling wolf sprang up in his place. Just a split second transformation. One that even the most skilled Belarian warrior would have been hard-pressed to recreate. They wrestled there a moment longer, locked in a writhing tangle of teeth and claws, then sprang apart at the same instant—shooting across the field.

It was utterly terrifying. And utterly exhilarating at the same time.

As many times as the princess had shifted, she had yet to test her new skills against another wolf. And while they may have been standing outside her own palace—a place where just yesterday the entire city had united in chanting her name—Seth wasn't pulling any punches.

From the second they collided again, she was fighting for her life.

The rest of the world faded away as they zeroed in on each other, unaware that the others had stopped what they were doing to watch from the side. Several cautionary arrows tried to fly between them, but they were moving at such speed that even Cosette held her fire. At any rate, there was something oddly beautiful about it— so the last thing she'd want to do was slow them down.

Vampires were fluid, the fae were pure grace, but fighting as a wolf landed somewhere in between. The pair leapt and dove, collided and detached, tumbled and flew, all with the same ceaseless momentum, all without ever missing a stride. It reminded Evie of the dancing master at her mother's castle, a man she had aged into early retirement but who had tortured her for three long years before that happened—clapping in a strict rhythm as she struggled to learn the steps.

The punishment then was a slap on the wrist.

The punishment here was much more painful.

She let out a sharp yelp as Seth caught her off balance, snapping punishingly at her shoulder before she fell back into stride. There was a compulsive movement on the other side of the arena as Asher took a step forward, but he caught himself just as quickly, watching with quiet interest.

No sooner had she landed than the wolf came at her again—latching on this time with a hard grip on the back of her neck. She cried out again, trying to shake him, then abruptly threw all her momentum backwards in a move her father had showed her, knocking him right off his feet.

His eyes twinkled in appreciation. She beamed in silent pride.

Round and round they tumbled, snickering with canine laughter and crashing about like a couple of pups. At one point he threw all his weight on top of her, refusing to allow her up until she found a way to dislodge him by herself. It was a painful lesson. One that took time.

She clawed and thrashed, but to no avail. She tried playing dead—prompting a chorus of laughter from her friends. At last she pitched herself forward, landing a bite on the side of his neck.

Victory!

With a triumphant howl she flew across the grass…only to find they were no longer alone.

The doors of the palace had opened and Dylan had frozen dead still on the steps. It took her a moment to interpret his expression, then all at once it clicked.

The King of Belaria had never seen his daughter as a wolf.

Her momentum stalled out abruptly, and her heart pounded unevenly in her chest. In a blind panic she almost shifted back on the spot, but found herself mortified by the prospect of nudity.

They stared at each for other a long moment, then she did the next best thing.

She took a running leap towards him...and came down on his chest. "Seven hells!"

It was more satisfying than she could have possibly imagined. For the first time in her life, the princess was stronger than the king. He stumbled backwards with the force of it, shaking with laughter, then she started thrashing around and he was knocked straight off his feet.

The two of them tumbled over the marble before the wolf came out on top. She stood there gloating a moment, then decided magnanimously to spare him, licking up the side of his face.

Only then did she see the council of advisors standing just behind. *...shit.*

"Congratulations, Sire...it's a wolf."

The rest of them laughed politely at Atticus' teasing, while the king pushed gracefully to his feet. His eyes twinkled as he reached out a hand, running his fingers through her glossy fur.

"It certainly is."

Their parents were coming down the steps just a few seconds behind them. There was something strange about the timing, as if they'd been waiting first for the council to depart.

Dylan waved them away quickly as the children raced towards them as well.

"Only in Belaria..." Asher murmured, shaking his head with a grin.

He still hadn't released the fae, opting to drag the prince behind him. By now, Ellanden had stopped trying to free himself and was hoping to simply expire on the lawn.

"What's this?" Cassiel asked with a faint smile, eyes flickering over his despondent son.

"A lesson in manners," Asher replied. "But I think he's learned it by now."

He dropped the fae's ankle as Evie bounded amongst the rest of them, showing off her new ability and taking great pleasure in striking each one with her tail. When at last she finished, she bounded back to the pile of clothes she'd left in the arena. Seth was already dressed and waiting, returning with her to the steps with a slightly dazed look on his face.

It wasn't difficult to read his expression, eyes flickering between the two groups. One set had trained the other. Given what he'd just seen from the children, he couldn't begin to imagine...

The others were already on the same page.

"So you grew up sparring against each other as well, right?" Freya asked, staring excitedly between the young monarchs. While the shifter might have kept such questions to himself, the witch had no such filter. "It's how you practice?"

Cassiel's eyes drifted to the girl, lingering there appraisingly.

It was hard to forget the rather shocking image he'd seen in the woods, yet it was impossible not to warm to the child as well. Quite possibly because she reminded him of another lovely young Kreo with a penchant for speaking her mind.

"Not all of us grew up together," he finally answered, glancing past her to where Dylan and Kailas were already testing out the swords. "Some of us haven't grown up at all. But yes, we've spent years sparring with each other. It's how the children learned."

The witch nodded with enormous eyes.

"So, who's the best of you?" she asked bluntly. "You must have tested it. Who would win in a fight between..." she pointed to the first person in sight, "...you and Kailas?"

Cosette gave her a sharp pinch. "Have you *no* manners at all?"

Cassiel's eyes sparkled with amusement as he glanced at the Damaris prince. Over the years, the initial animosity between them had given way to genuine affection. An affection that was only slightly dampened when Kailas did the unforgivable and made Serafina his bride.

"I would," he said calmly.

If he wasn't a dragon.

Evie squinted up at him with a grin. "What about you and my mother?"

There was a slight pause.

"I would," Cassiel said again. Though this time, he kept his eyes on the ground.

Katerina's eyebrows lifted as she paused to examine her nails. "Is that right?"

The nails started flaming.

"In hand to hand combat, there is no comparison," he replied dismissively.

"What about me?"

The others turned as Aidan jogged down the steps, murmuring something in Dylan's ear before joining the rest of them, eyes twinkling with a secret smile.

Cassiel looked at him appraisingly. "I don't know," he finally confessed. "Again—probably me."

The vampire flashed a grin, and for a moment Evie was reminded very strongly of both their sons. It was fortunate they hadn't left the palace sooner...they would not have approved.

"You really think so?"

"I've slaughtered many of your kind before. Though I'm sure you could last much longer than the others," Cassiel added graciously. "Keep dreaming, little one. Your day will come."

Little one?

A chorus of laughter followed the pronouncement as the rest of them broke into separate conversation, occupying themselves with the weapons and imagining such a pairing themselves.

"You're oddly quiet." Asher sidled up to Ellanden with a boyish grin. "You really think your father could beat mine?"

The fae glared impressively, still picking blades of grass from his hair. "I think my father should hold him by the foot for ten hours, until half of his body goes numb…"

Evie bounced past them obliviously, catching Seth by the arm.

"Do you want to keep practicing?" she asked in a rush. The adrenaline hadn't yet faded and she was desperate to get back onto the field. "Or has the audience got you scared off?"

Instead of answering, he glanced after the departing council. The garrison was just a short ways behind. "Actually, I was…I was hoping to ask for a commission in the infantry."

He said it quietly, but the words carried all the same.

"You were?" Cosette looked up suddenly, whitening in shock. "Why would…" She took a step closer, lowering her voice. "I would never see you. Why would you not fight alongside us?"

The question hung between them, though she was the only one who didn't understand.

In a flash, the shifter's words on the balcony echoed in Evie's ears. *There are protocols to this sort of thing. Places of privilege, levels of rank. I cannot be standing in the same hallway as my king.*

Her eyes softened as she understood the words he hadn't said.

I cannot fall in love with another king's daughter. Not without proving myself first.

Dylan glanced between them, then gestured the boy forward.

"A commission in the infantry," he repeated. "Why would you ask them at the garrison, when you could speak directly to me?"

"I didn't…I would never wish to…" The shifter's cheeks flamed in embarrassment as he dropped his gaze. "I'm sure you have far more important things to do with your time."

The king's eyes softened as they swept over the boy. Skin hardened by the elements. Hands callused from a sword. It was everything he missed about life as a ranger.

Then they drifted a little higher, to the woodland princess standing by his side.

"A commission is neither unimportant, nor beneath my time," he said briskly, taking off his cloak. "For that matter, it's something we can take care of right here."

The young shifter froze where he stood, utterly stunned. It wasn't until the vampire nudged him gently forward that he realized the others were waiting for him to speak.

"Th-thank you," he stammered, glancing around nervously. "What must I do?"

"To earn a place in the Belarian army?" Dylan threw a grin over his shoulder. "You must fight, of course. Good thing we have this handy arena."

Seth nodded automatically, then froze all at once. "What...*you?*"

There could be no greater nightmare, but it seemed the decision was already made. As he spoke, the others were drifting casually towards the grassy field to watch from the sidelines.

"Best of luck." Kailas clapped Dylan's shoulder, as if his brother-in-law was doing him a personal favor. "You're welcome to apply for a position in the High Kingdom's infantry as well."

"I'll write your mother a letter explaining what happened." Ellanden teased, forgetting his own indignity on the battlefield as he prepared to watch another. "It will be beautiful. She can read it to your sisters for years to come."

The shifter paled, fighting the urge to grab after him. "Wait, but I don't—"

"Here." Freya popped up in front of him, extending the flask. It hung between them a moment, then she retreated at the look on his face. "Just thought I'd offer..."

"But surely this isn't customary," he muttered to no one in particular, running a frazzled hand back through his hair. "Not every common foot soldier must fight the king."

"Not every common foot soldier just bit the king's daughter," Evie said unfeelingly, pairing it with a wicked smile. "Don't worry, I'm sure he didn't see."

With that, the rest of the boy's allies vanished into the arena. In the seconds that followed, he came to the profound realization that they'd never been allies at all.

There was a fleeting moment when he considered taking off into the forest. There was a pack waiting in the mountains. People he loved and trusted, who didn't require his untimely death.

Then he took a deep breath and turned towards the arena instead, gazing past the others to the silhouette of a slender girl with long ivory hair.

Here goes nothing...

Chapter 11

"That was INCREDIBLE! I couldn't have done better MYSELF!"

Evie sat next to Seth at dinner that night, proudly recapping each of his best moments—as if she'd had a hand in shaping that talent herself. The exhibition between him and the king had lasted much longer than expected, and it was already dark by the time they'd made it back inside.

"Can you please stop?" he asked quietly, cheeks burning with a blush. It was a good effort, but he couldn't stop grinning. The fae princess by his side helped a great deal. The ale helped as well.

When he and Dylan had first stepped into the arena, it had been a little touch and go.

The young shifter was paralyzed with nerves, and the king was highly aware that he could do no serious damage without hearing an earful from both his beloved niece and his wife. It wasn't until the end of the first round that he realized the boy could hold his own.

It wasn't exactly an even fight, but it was an interesting one.

The time Seth had spent fending off the world's monsters in Tarnaq had polished a skillset that had already been well-developed by the Red Hand. The result was a rather eclectic style that could rise to meet any occasion, flexible enough to improvise with various weaponry, but anchored by the raw talent that lay at its core. Evie remembered being blown away the first time she'd seen him fight in the arena—such nightmares had been thrown against him, but he'd driven them back with a smile. A warrior and a showman. One who didn't delight in bloodshed, but knew how to play to a crowd. She remembered thinking that her father would have appreciated the talent.

This went a bit beyond that. The man was seriously impressed.

"Where did you learn this?" he'd asked in amazement, levelling a devastating blow at the child that was returned so quickly he'd had to step back to avoid getting struck.

"Here and there," Seth had modestly replied.

In the beginning, he'd had a great deal of difficulty with the concept of raising a hand against his sovereign. Dylan had helped him past that rather quickly by having no such hesitations himself.

They battled on for a good twenty minutes before the king finally set down his blade. The rest of them assumed the fight was over. The sun was getting lower, both men were panting, and the second Dylan took a step towards the weapons rack Seth let out a quiet prayer of thanks.

But the Belarian army didn't often fight as men. They fought as wolves.

It happened faster than anyone could make sense of—the instant the king set down his sword he leapt straight back at shifter, transforming mid-flight. It was a test all by itself. One that Seth passed in the nick of time. No sooner had he made the shift himself than the wolf barreled into him, sending them both tumbling violently over the ground.

If it was possible, the fight took on a new level. Both wolves were lithe and agile, not like some of the hulking monsters that prowled in the guard. And both had the same acrobatic quality, as if some inner part of them was always suspended, ready to take off and fly.

They battled back and forth over the clearing, tearing into each other in a stunning display of skill, until there was a sudden flash of claws as Seth struck the king across the face.

A sharp cry echoed into the evening as the clearing went suddenly still.

The adults looked on with a touch of surprise, while the children leapt to their feet. Cosette had gone pale as a ghost, both hands clamped over her face as she peered through her fingers.

Both wolves had shifted back immediately.

While Seth fell to his knees in mortified submission, Dylan lifted a hand to his face. He stared at the young man for a moment, a peculiar look in his eyes.

Then his lips curved into a smile.

"Cass...come here for a second."

The fae had been watching with interest, and when his friend called he pushed lightly to his feet, moving across the grass. Cosette stood up as well, hurrying to join them.

"Uncle Dylan—" she had tried to intervene.

"Trust me," he winked. "This will help you in the long run."

He wasn't wrong...

"The boy is a treasure," Cassiel declared, pouring him another goblet of ale. "Not since Dylan was a teenager have I seen such talent. He'll make the Belarian army proud."

It was said to the entire table, but directed a bit more specifically towards Kailas. As it happened, the crown prince of the High Kingdom was the only person to remain unimpressed.

"That's fantastic," he muttered sarcastically, "my measuring stick for all my daughter's potential suitors—whether they'll make the Belarian army proud."

Evie snorted into her drink, while her father shrugged.

"There are worse ways to measure."

"A trial by fire," Adelaide chided good-naturedly. "You should all be ashamed."

The older queen was the only one who hadn't the stomach to watch the initiation with the rest of them. She'd looked down from the balcony instead, flinching with every blow.

"Nonsense," Dylan countered with a wink. "The boy exceeded our every expectation. I foresee great things for him ahead..."

The crown prince sank lower in his chair.

"You must be patient, Kailas," Cassiel advised sagely. "Approach it with an open mind."

Kailas shot him a dark look.

"Because you were so known for that yourself?" he snapped caustically. "Because you were so known for your open-minded patience when I was courting Sera?"

The fae's handsome face went blank. "When in the *world* did you court Sera?"

"...you are impossible."

"I must have honestly blocked it out."

Evie watched as they dissolved into their usual argument with a grin before turning to her father. The man had a shining welt across one cheek, but was looking undeniably pleased.

"So how was the meeting this morning?" she asked quietly, deliberately hiding the question amidst a sea of conversation. "Did the council agree to come with us? To join in our fight?"

He started nodding, but then something about the question made him pause. His eyes shot across the table to where Aidan was watching, then he cleared his face with a quick smile.

"Belaria is with us." He took a deep drink of his ale. "Or they will be tomorrow," he added off-handedly. "There's an official ceremony, then we'll be heading off."

She nodded slowly, watching him all the while. "What's the ceremony?"

"Atticus immediately relinquished control back to me, but it's customary after such a long absence to allow for any challengers before taking up the throne."

"A ridiculous tradition," Katerina muttered.

"A point of cultural pride," he husband corrected with a smile.

The princess was simply stunned.

"Challengers?" she repeated in astonishment. "So if they fight you and win...they get the crown?"

Ellanden pushed slowly to his feet. Asher pulled him back down.

"Pretty much," her father replied, throwing a quick grin at the impulsive fae. "Any time, sweetheart. I won't even make you wear shoes."

Freya's eyes narrowed, perhaps sensing an opportunity to even the playing field in one fell swoop. "Can you use magic?"

Tanya snorted in amusement, while Dylan laughed out loud.

"Well I wasn't expecting to find any challengers at this table, but since you're all so disturbingly eager—the chance is only for the wolves."

The witch slumped in her chair, muttering at her plate. "...discrimination..."

"So after the ceremony, we're off to the High Kingdom?" Evie asked, wondering silently if either of her parents would allow her to fly. It was a long journey over some uninviting terrain, but it was just a few short hours by dragon. "You know, I could always speed things up—"

"We're not going to the High Kingdom," Katerina interrupted, staring at her plate. Aidan glanced pointedly from across the table, and she looked up so suddenly it was as though he was speaking inside her head. "We're going to Taviel."

Ellanden perked up immediately, but Evie was confused.

"But what about the Belarian army?" she asked. "They'd be travelling for months, in the wrong direction...by sea? Surely they can't come with us. And what about the High Kingdom? Or the Kreo, for that matter? I assumed we'd go to Taviel last, just because it's the farthest away."

It was a rare thing for the princess to make such sense, especially when she was dealing with logistics. She'd expected these answers to be simple, but neither of her parents could meet her eyes.

"The leaders of each of those kingdoms will meet us in the Ivory City," Cassiel swept in for a quick save. "Whatever discussions we have in terms of moving forward can happen there."

Whatever discussions?

The friends exchanged a bewildered glance.

The realm no longer operated in terms of individual kingdoms. Since the Battle of the Dunes, it had functioned as a whole. The decision of one would stand for the rest of them. Hence the term: *alliance*. If Belaria had already gotten on board, what else was there to discuss?

She wanted to ask, but something about her mother's expression made her hesitate. In the end, she dropped her eyes back to her plate with a quick nod.

Perhaps Seth had been right with his earlier assessment.

Perhaps she should have been at that meeting after all.

THE CEREMONY IN THE morning was faster than the princess could have believed, possibly because most everyone standing behind her on the palace steps had been recently informed there was a vengeful dragon on the prowl and time was suddenly of the essence.

She stood on the dais beside her parents, watching as Atticus went through all the necessary proclamations—delivering a surprisingly poignant speech, considering they were pressed for time.

His eyes shone when he discussed the return of their beloved leader. It was a joy made all the brighter because of the pain of his absence. Katerina reached secretly to take Dylan's hand.

By the time the councilman made the obligatory pause for any challengers, her heart was pounding so fast she half-expected to hear a chorus of voices. If her friends had been allowed all the ale they'd wanted the previous evening, some of those voices might have been their own.

But there wasn't a sound in the pavilion. Not a single breath. The moment the crown was lowered onto his head, every citizen of Belaria bowed their heads in the same reverent hush.

"Long live the king!" Atticus called from the podium.

The sound of his voice propelled the people to their feet.

"Long live the king!"

THERE WASN'T REALLY a point in packing.

Like those lingering houseguests who never really left, each of the friends had stashed things in the palaces of the others. Everything from food to books. From clothes to weapons. No need to bring anything if everything was already there. But still, Evie found herself in her alone in her childhood bedroom, throwing random things into a bag.

"The last bags we packed got burned in a fire," a voice called from the doorway. "Might be safer at this point to travel light."

There was a rush of air, then Asher was there—spinning her around for a sudden kiss.

"Careful," she gasped, glancing behind him towards the door. He hadn't even bothered to close it. "My parents are right down the—" His tongue crept into her mouth and she broke off mid-sentence, stretching to the tips of her toes as her fingers slid into his ebony hair.

Considering how remarkably attentive their parents had been, she'd been amazed they'd kept their little secret thus far. They hadn't exactly been careful—kissing just a stone's throw away from the palace steps. It didn't look like Asher wanted to be careful right now.

He tapped the door shut with one hand while carrying her to the bed with the other.

"Are you insane?" she whispered with a giggle as he dropped her carelessly onto the mattress, stretching his body over hers. "My parents are right down the hall."

The guards were right outside the residence. The dungeon was just a few floors beneath that.

"And soon they'll be down the hall in Taviel," he murmured, trailing kisses down the side of her neck. "They're always nearby—what's the difference?" He kissed her silent before she could answer, eyes twinkling with a mischievous smile. "I can be quiet..."

Except I know that you can't.

They tangled together a moment longer, just long enough for her to lose sight of the reasons not to, just long enough for her resolve to crumble. It came back as she stared up into the eyes of a childhood painting—inconveniently timed with the moment his hand began sneaking up her dress.

"The unicorn is watching me."

He tensed, then glanced up at her. "Please don't call it that."

She snorted with laughter, sliding out from under him to lean back against the ornate headboard. He watched her a moment, then settled lightly by her side.

"What's the matter?"

The smile faded, and she tensed without really knowing why.

"Nothing," she said quickly, nervous to have offended him. "It's just my parents actually *are* just a few steps down the—"

He held up a quick hand, shaking his head with a twinkling smile. "I couldn't care less about that. And we should be careful," he added chidingly. "Everly, I don't know if you realize, but your *parents* are just a few steps down the hall."

She smacked him with a grin, but it faded the longer they sat there.

"Seriously," he pressed a kiss to her knuckles, staring into her eyes, "what's wrong? You've been like this since your father's re-coronation. Even longer, you've been like this since dinner—"

"Sometimes I wish we were back on our own."

He fell perfectly silent, staring up at her in surprise. "You wish—"

"Not...not *actually* on our own," she stammered as a guilty blush colored her cheeks. "I just don't..." She trailed off in frustration, biting the inside of her lip. "When did we start keeping secrets? When did we start doing everything by committee? Why are we going to Taviel first?"

He leaned back with a thoughtful sigh, pushing back his hair. "I've been asking myself the same thing."

She looked at him carefully, desperately hoping that was true. "There have just been these weird moments, Asher. Nothing noticeable—just a look or a word—but there have been these *moments*. Something's missing here. Something's wrong."

He stared back at her, wanting very much to deny it but knowing all the while it was true. A few seconds passed, each dragging longer than the last. Then his shoulders rose in a helpless shrug.

"Maybe they're protecting us."

"Protecting us," she echoed, unable to do anything but repeat it. "How do you mean?"

He released her hand and began playing with the bedspread. He then moved his attention to his sleeve, then his wrist. Then it was his finger. The same one his father had bitten just days before.

"We didn't make a clean getaway," he finally answered. "We left things messy. Why do you think they've been in meetings since we arrived? Would it be so unlikely if there were feelings of discontent? If there were things they weren't telling us? Logistics that could only cause us pain?"

She took a deep breath, then nodded. It made a lot more sense when he phrased it like that.

"It just felt so much easier when it was the six of us," she admitted softly, stopping that endless fidgeting as she reached again to take his hand. "When we discussed something, it would be right there in the open. When we made a plan, we'd set off right then to see it through. I just hate putting that control in the hands of other people. Even if they're *our* people. It's like we've been sent back to the nursery, just waiting for them to return and tell us what happens next."

He stared at her a moment longer, then pulled her gently into his lap—kissing the side of her head as he rocked them back and forth. "That's why you're going to make an incredible queen."

She laughed shortly, leaning against him. "Because of my compulsion to micro-manage?"

He grinned into her hair. "I was going to say your inability to delegate. But, yes—precisely that."

They stayed like that for a while longer, each playing back those same fateful moments in their heads. Each wondering how they might fit together, how they might play a part..

Belaria is with us.

"It's like they're talking about one kingdom at a time," she whispered. "Like the crown was the only thing holding the realm together and even with something like this...they aren't united."

He stiffened beneath her, then pressed another kiss to her head. "That's what we're here to do."

She nodded silently, cuddling into him.

Why do I get the feeling it's not going to be that simple?

THE PRINCESS AND THE vampire abandoned the idea of packing, and simply lay in bed together as the sun travelled slowly across the sky. They watched the shadows streaming in from the window, and listened to the soldiers chattering back and forth as they patrolled beneath the castle wall.

"You know the thing about a bond?" he said suddenly, startling her back to the present. "I can literally feel when you're still stressing; when you can't let something go."

She glanced up at him in surprise, blushing at the same time. It had been quiet so long, she'd half-thought he'd fallen asleep. She didn't know he'd been lying there, worrying about her worrying.

"I'm sorry," she said automatically, trying to straighten up, "I wasn't trying to—"

"No need to be sorry," he interrupted lightly. "There's a lot going on. You're right to be stressing." There was a pause. "I just think we should have taken our clothes off after all..."

The tension vanished as she burst out laughing—feeling his arms tighten as she buried her face in his chest. Every time she tried to stop it just got worse, until he was laughing as well.

"I say it only from a psychological perspective," he defended himself. "It isn't good to remain in such a state for long stretches of time."

She laughed even harder, rolling onto his chest. "What a martyr! You would do that for me?"

He nodded seriously, those enormous eyes taking up half his face. "I would do a great many things for you," he began, then coming to a sudden pause. "As long as you never reference any part of me as *the unicorn*. It's just a step too far—"

Fresh peals of laughter shook the bed as she forgot their previous distance and pushed on top of him, wrapping her legs around his waist. He sat up with her, cheeks flushed with that rare bit of color he got whenever the two were in bed. But before things could go any further he paused with an unexpectedly tender expression, pushing back the fiery locks of her hair.

"Whatever happens...I'll be right there beside you."

She pulled in a quick breath. "Do you promise?"

He stared into her eyes. "Always."

They kissed deeply, slowly. Then their hands started fidgeting beneath each other's clothing, and that kiss quickly heated into something more...at the precise moment the door pushed open.

"Asher, did you already—"

Aidan caught himself almost immediately, freezing in the frame.

His eyes lingered only a moment on Evie before drifting to his son. His quiet, reserved son, who was lit up in a way his father had never seen—his heart beating strong beneath her hands.

"Oh..." the vampire said softly, taking a step back. "I was overwhelmed by your return...I didn't see..."

The princess was frozen in horror, wracking her brain for something to say. But Asher didn't say anything. He simply stared back at his father, then reached down to take her hand.

"I'm sorry," Aidan said swiftly, backing into the hall. "The others are ready to leave. That's all I came to tell you."

He was gone a moment later, leaving the door swinging in his wake.

There was a split second of silence, then both teenagers extracted themselves at the same time—smoothing down hair and gathering their composure before glancing into each other's eyes.

"Do you think he's going to..." Evie trailed off, unable to say the rest.

Asher stared at the door then shook his head. "No, he wouldn't. Our secret's safe."

She followed his gaze with a belated shudder.

For now...

The two finished packing quickly and headed towards the common room. Sure enough, the others were already waiting, gathered in a loose circle by the door.

No one looked up as they entered, no one said anything strange.

It actually looked as though they had been conveniently distracted. As it turned out, not everyone was nervous to be going to Taviel. Some people were downright giddy instead.

To put it lightly.

Ellanden's moods had always been contagious, and that day he didn't disappoint.

Of all the rest of them, he was the one standing closest to the door—bag held firmly in hand, cheerfully monologuing at anyone foolish enough to come within sight.

"—take a while to get there, I'll grant you, but what's a few hours by dragon in the grand scheme of things? It's been said that until you've laid eyes on the Ivory City you haven't really lived. *I'm* one of the people who says that. I actually think I might have made it up—"

He'd grabbed Seth by the arm and was leaning casually against him, in a way he usually reserved for Asher or the princess herself. Of course, he didn't seem to notice. He was so caught up, the shifter could have set his clothes on fire and it would have taken a moment to respond.

"—but that's only the outer rim of the island. When you get further inside—"

His parents were watching from the kitchen. They could have stood there and watched him for hours. Even the shifter was smiling, eyes flickering between the hand wrapped around his jacket and the fae's boot, which was bouncing at the speed of light.

"—not expressly forbidden, but I'll be staying in my old room. Oh, hey guys!" He lit up as Asher and Evie slipped into the room, still chattering away although no one else was listening. "So will both of you, I'm sure the quarters haven't changed. Unless you're staying together now—"

He caught himself suddenly as a silent hush fell over the room.

A dozen faces turned and a dozen pairs of eyes locked on the princess' face. Her own mother was chief among them, staring with an expression that was nothing short of shocked.

The fae glanced around guiltily, lowering his voice. "I'm sorry...have you not told them yet?"

Evie's eyes snapped shut.

Turns out, they were listening after all.

Chapter 12

The best thing about flying by dragon...was that there were plenty of places to jump.

Evie sat stiffly between her uncle's shoulder blades, pretending she didn't notice how the rest of them were giving her a graciously wide berth. 'Wide berth' being a relative term, when all your loved ones were sitting on the back of the same dragon. She was still close enough to see every astonished expression, to catch all those silent exchanges as they soared through the clouds. She was still sitting close enough to flick tiny vengeful sparks at the back of Ellanden's hair.

"Stop that," Dylan chided, swatting her hand with a curious frown. "What's gotten into you?"

In the brief yet tragic revelation of the princess and the vampire's love life, there had been just one small mercy: her father hadn't been in the room.

She shot him a sideways glance, forcing a pained smile. "You know...just passing the time."

Just calling it 'time' was generous. The princess felt as though she'd slipped into some kind of purgatory ages ago. While travelling by dragon might have been a thousand times faster than taking a ship, it was still a long journey to Taviel. The Fae's prized city had been built at a deliberate distance, during a time when older and more terrible monsters roamed the skies.

It was said to be safe because no single dragon could ever reach it. No matter how savage and determined they might be, at some point they'd tire and simply fall into the sea.

It had taken the Damaris twins all of five minutes to create a loophole. They wouldn't travel to the Ivory City with just one dragon. They'd travel there with two.

...but not three.

The siblings had already traded places several times. It was a stunningly acrobatic display, one that required a great deal of faith as well as some physical dexterity from their passengers. But no matter how many times the princess begged to be allowed into the more menacing of the roles she had been unanimously banned, leaving her sulking in silence on her uncle's back.

...playing a terrible game of "Who's going to tell the ranger?".

"If it's any consolation, I'm excited to get there myself," Dylan confided, nudging her with a little grin. "The others are being freakishly quiet, and you have been nothing short of a nightmare."

She tried to smile again, then turned to him instead. "*Please* let me fly."

"No."

"You let Mother do it."

"He doesn't *let* me do anything," Katerina chimed in dangerously.

"Your mother and I fight often," Dylan explain calmly. "She would be an acceptable person to lose. You are my darling daughter. You must remain safe at all costs."

She settled back with a scowl, restlessly tapping a finger against her leg. Asher was sitting as far away from her as possible, but every so often she'd feel the weight of those dark eyes.

Along with *everyone* else's.

"What if she came with me?" she blurted in desperation. "Come on, we have to be close."

He opened his mouth to refuse again, but this time Katerina pushed to her feet.

"Just let her, Dylan. She's right—we're only a handful of miles away."

How they could tell, the princess would never know. But she beamed with delight when her father nodded curtly—waving her dismissively over the side. With a little shriek of glee she kissed his cheek, took off her cloak, then leapt into the air—escaping the awkward situation altogether.

Of course, that's when she discovered something about dragons.

So...are we going to talk about this?

The princess almost fell out of the sky.

No sooner had she made the transformation, curling into herself and reemerging in a writhing ball of flames, than her mother's voice echoed innocently inside her head.

Literally...*inside* her head.

DID YOU JUST SAY THAT?! She shrieked at the top of her mental voice, unsure how these things might project. *CAN YOU HEAR MY THOUGHTS?!*

The fiery dragon on her left trembled with what might have been laughter.

Yes, darling; there's no need to shout.

No need to shout.

She'd left the others mid-journey, actually jumped off a dragon's back over the middle of the ocean, just to escape the awkward tension. Now here she was...every thought an open book.

It'll be fine, she said to herself, forgetting for a moment that the others could hear. *Just don't think about anything personal. Don't think about Asher. Don't think about the bell tower. Don't think about what happened underneath the bell tower with Asher. Don't think about what almost happened again right before we—*

Please, Kailas inserted mildly, *please don't do this while I'm here.*

The princess cast him a frenzied look, while her thoughts grew manic—spiraling faster and faster away. When she realized she couldn't control them, she decided to silence them instead.

Can I drown myself? What if I flew straight down into the water? Would I float back up again?

Katerina shot her a look that was a little hard to define.

Sweetheart, can you please stop talking about drowning yourself?

I'm not TALKING about it!

She tried to scream out loud, but all that came out was a rather anemic-sounding cough. A cough that still packed plenty of fire—as she was quickly told by the angry mob on Kailas' back.

I hate it when they jump around like that. He rippled his shoulders with a hint of irritation, trying not to squirm. *It's like ants crawling on your skin.*

This. Is. So. Weird.

It's not weird, honey. Katerina flew up alongside her, inadvertently shading her daughter with the curve of her wing. *It's something Kailas and I discovered the first night we shifted at the same time. I always assumed that when you managed to shift it was a connection we would share as well.*

Evie cast her a quick look, gliding over the water.

It was one of the things she loved most about her mother—that unfailing sense of optimism. It was never a question of *if* her daughter would shift. It was a foregone conclusion.

Perhaps this was why she consented to answer a few coaxing questions.

So...you and Asher?

Yeah.

And...that's been going on for a while?

Yeah.

Okay...anything else I should know?

The princess paused.

I'm in love with him.

Both dragons glanced over at the same time, then continued flying. It was hard to tell with the scales and overall sense of menace, but she could have sworn her mother had a little smile.

It vanished abruptly as the queen glanced over in panic.

Actually, sweetheart, there's something else I should tell you.

The princess eyed her warily.

What?

There was a terrible pause.

...your Uncle Aidan can hear these thoughts as well.

THE REMAINDER OF THE flight to Taviel was as invigorating as it was brief. The princess had decided to murder her mother the second they touched down on dry land, but her uncle seemed determined to distract his tortured niece in whatever way he knew how.

In the world of dragons, this turned out to be by dumping his passengers onto the back of his sister, then making a general fool of himself for her own entertainment.

She snorted with a burst of involuntary laughter as he streaked past her again—flying in such tight circles that the rest of them were constantly having to adjust their own flight path just to avoid ramming into him. If they were anywhere within sight of the Ivory City, the Fae must have been staring in horror—convinced the dragon had lost its mind. On the flip side, her own father was so beside himself with excitement and jealousy she was surprised he didn't try to leap aboard himself.

There was another 'close call' and she finally reared back herself—twirling up in a deadly spiral before streaking down on him from above. It was a breathtaking display, one that took every bit of her rather limited concentration. But her uncle had years of extra practice to his name.

At the last possible second he whirled around to face her, grabbing hold with one of his giant talons and thrashing her playfully through the sky. When her mother let out a horrific growl, warning him to be careful, he released her in a flash and dove towards the ocean—surfacing a split-second later with a mouthful of water...that he proceeded to spit into his sister's face.

By this time, the princess was roaring with laughter (a rather terrifying sight, if one happened to be a dragon), while the rest of her family had sided vehemently against the prince. There were the usual profanities and threats of decapitation, but they seemed rather insignificant from such height.

When Kailas dove into the water once again, she was ready for him—hovering with an anticipatory smile just a few hundred feet above. She watched as he plunged into the waves then came tearing back out again, jaws open, shooting straight up from beneath—

I know you're there, child. I felt you coming.

A deep voice sounded in the princess' ears, echoes of the same words she'd heard before.

What chance do you think you have...against something like me?

The world tilted as she sucked in a faltering breath, closing her eyes ever so briefly against the sudden rush of air. She didn't realize she was falling until she hit the water. She didn't realize her uncle had saved her until he was setting her down on dry land.

...dry land?

They had arrived. They had made it to Taviel.

By the time she opened her eyes, she was already human. Her friends were racing towards her. Her mother had already shifted back and was draping a heavy cloak across her body.

"Evie?" She hovered above her, eyes tight with fear. "Honey—can you hear me?"

Can I hear you? Haven't we been talking this whole time?

The princess sat up slowly, lifting a hand to her forehead—realizing only belatedly that it was a hand instead of a wing. The sand on the beach was smooth and cool under her legs, a pale silt that crested around her with each faltering movement, as if to encase her there forever.

"Yeah, I can hear you," she murmured, wincing at a sudden throbbing in her temple. A few paces beyond them, the final dragon had disappeared and was hastily dressing as a man. "What just happened? I can't even remember—"

"Evie!"

To her great surprise it was Asher who reached her first, pushing straight through the others to kneel at the princess' side. His hands slipped behind her back and he lifted her gently, those dark eyes wild with concern as he smoothed back a tangle of her sandy hair.

"What happened?" he breathed, echoing her same question. "One second you were just playing with Kailas, but the next—"

He tensed suddenly as Dylan appeared on the ground beside him, breathless from the speed at which he'd streaked across the beach. "Sweetheart—are you all right?"

His hands reached automatically to steady her, only to find other hands already there.

"Thanks, Ash." He pushed the vampire aside distractedly. "I got it."

The rest of her family exchanged a silent look behind him as Asher froze in a moment of indecision, then slipped back to join the rest. Kailas was already racing towards them.

He was immediately struck by no fewer than five people.

"What the hell happened?!"

"You terrified her, that's what happened!" Katerina snapped, raising a handful of dragon fire to shove into her brother's face. He smothered it quickly in his own fist, kneeling beside them.

"I'm sorry, sweetheart." He reached past Dylan to squeeze her hand, those lovely dark eyes shining with concern. "I didn't mean to frighten you."

"You didn't," Evie answered quickly, trying to sit up. "It wasn't your fault. I was just..."

She trailed into silence as another group of people stepped onto the beach.

These weren't windswept or disheveled. Quite the opposite. An otherworldly poise defined their every motion as they came to a collective pause on the sand.

Her father lifted her quickly as the man in front stepped forward, his dark eyes sweeping across the band of travelers with what might have been the trace of a smile.

"That was quite the entrance," he murmured.

Then those eyes alighted upon Cassiel, and he sank into a respectful bow.

"Our lord has returned to us. Welcome home."

THE JOURNEY TO TAVIEL was indeed more subdued than their entrance to Belaria. There were no shouts or cheering, no deafening anthem of applause. It was subdued, but no less powerful.

And it seemed to continue a long way...

It was a bit of a trek from the beach to the Ivory City. The friends followed the delegation of fae who'd come to greet them, walking past all those places they'd grown up reading about in stories. Around the well of whispers, through the enchanted forest, up the misty mountain trail.

At every step, more fae melted out of the woods to meet them—saying not a word but bowing their heads in quiet deference, tracking every movement with those luminous, eternal eyes.

By the time they reached the famed gates, the princess had shivers racing up her arms.

"Is it always like this?" Freya whispered, unable to tear her eyes from the fae.

Evie considered a moment.

"Not too far off, actually. Just a bit lighter. Happier."

It was one of her strongest memories from childhood. Taviel had always been a happy place.

The witch wasn't the only one feeling anxious.

Despite their innate calm, the Fae often left the people around them feeling inexplicably nervous. Perhaps it was because there was no way to hide the differences between them. It created an unintentional feeling of exclusion, as if one was always watching from the outside.

The vampires were keeping their eyes down and taking measured steps amidst the others, trying not to appear as a threat. Adelaide was staring around in wonder, having never been there before, and Seth was walking so closely beside the princess he occasionally stepped on her feet.

"Sorry," he breathed for the third time, still glancing apprehensively around him. A part of him was dying to explore, while another part wanted to run straight back to the beach. "It's just…"

She squeezed his hand, holding back a little smile. "I know."

They wound their way quickly through the city, over a lattice-work of carved bridges and elegant houses, struggling to keep traction on the smooth alabaster streets. The sparkling water of no fewer than three sunlit rivers danced alongside them, splashing happily around corners and filling the air with occasional bursts of rainbow-tinted mist. It was enough to take one's breath away. Enough to soften even the most resistant heart, and leave one feeling pensive and overwhelmed.

Then all at once…it was over.

The friends came to a stop in the shadow of the ivory citadel, staring up at its gleaming towers as Leonor stepped forward and whispered a few words into Cassiel's ear. The fae listened to him in silence, nodding with a little frown, then summoned the attention of the others.

"They have prepared chambers for us," he said briskly. "Lavinia sent a message to let them know we were coming. The rest of you are welcome to settle in… I'll join you shortly."

After having the most difficult council meeting of my immortal life.

"…who's Lavinia?" Evie whispered to Asher.

"It's Ellanden's grandmother. Kreo side."

The princess' eyebrows shot up in astonishment.

"Gran has a *name*?"

They had always ever called her "Gran" or "Chief".

"That's very considerate, Leonor," Katerina said gratefully. "Thank you."

The young queen had always taken extra care to stay on good terms with the elder fae, ever since she'd made his life impossibly harder by refusing a marriage proposal to his prince.

He gave her a dry stare.

The fae had a long memory. And his people tended to hold grudges.

The others slipped past him in silence—Serafina and Cosette pausing only to give him a quick kiss on the cheek. Only Tanya broke the silence, clapping his arm with a tiny grin.

"Nice to see you, Leo."

The fae stiffened, as if it was a moniker they'd battled over many times, before melting into a breathtaking smile the moment her son stepped forward to take her place.

"*Ellanden.*"

The councilman embraced him affectionately, thawing with a kind of warmth the others had rarely seen. He leaned back after a moment, eyes lingering on the sun-kissed cheeks and wavy hair.

"You've grown."

The prince blushed, but didn't release him—his fingers were still curled around the man's sleeve. While the rest of his people would no doubt be told some official version of what happened, for this particular person he felt the need to say the words himself.

"I have so much to tell you," he murmured, staring almost nervously into the man's eyes. "I never intended..." He paused for a breath. "Might we speak later, Leonor? As we used to?"

The fae smiled again before gently steering him forward.

"We may speak as long as you wish."

He guided them through the arched doors and into an outer courtyard. From there, they ascended a winding staircase that led to the highest level of the pavilion—one that had assimilated seamlessly into the natural beauty of the mountain and remained effectively hidden from the rest.

The private quarters of the House of Elénarin.

No matter the splendor of her own palaces, the princess had to admit the Fae's ancestral home was without question the loveliest of them all. Quite possibly because it wasn't a palace but a mere extension of the city, which was a mere extension of the waterfalls themselves—a shimmering beacon rising from the water, the look of which was pure fantasy, beckoning the next ages to come.

"Do you have everything you need?" Leonor asked stiffly. The princess glanced around to see him looking at the vampires with a distrust he made little effort to hide.

Aidan and Asher were the first vampires ever allowed in the Ivory City. Their parents had considered this a great honor. The children had considered it a matter of convenience, as it would have been impossible otherwise to play. Over the years, most of the fae had warmed to them.

Others had not.

"I believe we do." Aidan inclined his head with a smile. No matter the severity of his treatment, the vampire was never anything but polite to the fae. "Thank you, Leonor."

The elder nodded swiftly, then swept back down the steps—no doubt off to instruct the kitchens to send hunters into the forest, lest they start losing townsfolk instead.

The friends stared until he was gone, then turned back to each other.

...time to unpack.

※

FOR THE NEXT FEW HOURS Evie and the others settled into their new chambers, basking in the serenity and trying to ignore how much it resembled the alpine villa they'd left just few days before.

It looks like it, she thought, throwing open her bedroom window. *But it doesn't feel like it at all...*

Her fingers wrapped around the frame as she leaned into the sunlight—closing her eyes and pulling in a deep breath of that sweet-scented air. There were always flowers blooming in Taviel; it didn't matter if those flowers happened to be in season or not. She'd heard her father say once that poets and artists used to make pilgrimages to the city from every corner of the realm—searching for light and inspiration. She could imagine such a thing quite easily herself.

"Lovely day." Asher knocked twice on the doorframe, then stepped inside—leaving it wide open behind him. "Then again, it's always lovely here. I can see why Landi doesn't like to leave."

The princess stepped away from the window with a smile, noting the open door.

"Want to close that?" she teased, sitting down on the bed. "Come and join me?"

He flashed a grin, but stayed right where he was—leaning back against her vanity with his long legs stretched out in front of him. "I think it's probably best if I keep a little distance. It was bad enough with your father on the beach..."

He trailed off suddenly, flashing a look of concern. "What happened back there? Did you faint?"

Her face stilled, then she dropped her eyes to the floor. "I'm not sure...possibly." She hesitated again, wondering how much to tell him. "You know those dreams I had of the dragon?"

Easier to say 'the dragon' instead of calling him by name.

Asher nodded slowly, watching carefully from across the room.

"I heard his voice again...like an echo." She shivered in the balmy sunshine, folding her arms across her chest. "Sometimes it's hard to believe we'll actually have to face him."

For what felt like a lifetime they had been circling towards each other, travelling roads that would eventually collide. It was easier not to think of it. It was easier to focus only on the stone.

The vampire's face tightened, then he crossed the room without thinking to sit beside her on the bed. One hand swept back her long hair as the other tilted up her chin.

"When that happens, we'll face him together."

She nodded briskly, then shot him a quick look. "...and he'll eat us."

There was a long stretch of silence.

Then the vampire pointed to the window.

"Go," he instructed. "You need more time in the sun."

She burst out laughing, falling back on the bed. "I'm serious—"

"So am I," he insisted, pulling her up again. "You need to let this place work its magic on you. No more talk of dismemberment and death."

And speaking of...

"May I come in?"

The two glanced up in unison as Ellanden paused uncertainly in the doorway.

He was holding a stack of blankets, though they were clearly just a prop. In a last-second rush of nerves, he'd picked up a potted plant as well and was balancing it awkwardly atop the pile.

"Just thought I'd bring you some things..." he stammered, flashing a tight smile and avoiding their eyes. "Do you, uh...do you guys have everything you need?"

They stared in silence, watching the panic take hold.

Remorse didn't come easily to the Fae. Neither did the concept of forgiveness. Caught in a tangle between the two their friend floundered awkwardly, wondering again why he'd taken the plant.

"I sent for some blood from the kitchens. At first they thought I meant *bread*, but we got it cleared up and it should be here soon. I remembered that you like it better warm..."

He trailed into silence, or perhaps he simply ran out of breath.

"What's with the ficus?" Asher finally replied.

The prince's face went blank.

"...pardon?"

The vampire gestured to the plant.

"Oh—right." Ellanden blushed and set it gingerly on the dresser, leaving a trail of dirty water in its wake. "That was just…doesn't matter. I was actually hoping to find you and…"

His shoulders wilted in defeat.

"…I'm very sorry."

They took a single look at his face and their anger vanished. It was quite possibly the first time he'd ever said the words. Between that and the ficus, he was ready to break.

"Don't worry about it," Evie replied, glancing at his muddy hands with an affectionate smile. "You didn't do anything on purpose."

Asher leaned back with an exasperated grin. "It had to happen sooner or later—"

"Please," the fae interrupted quickly, "let me say this."

The others paused in surprise, caught off guard by his tone.

"I had no idea the rest of them didn't know," he continued earnestly, "because how could they not see it? This isn't some passing attraction, a random fling…the two of you are in love."

Asher and Evie glanced at each other, unsure what to say, while the fae's eyes gentled with an expression they'd never quite seen. He stared for a moment, lingering on each one.

"In the beginning, I was hoping you'd get over it," he admitted quietly. "I thought such a thing would divide us, but I couldn't have been more wrong. It's as though the two of you were simply waiting for each other. It's provided a kind of balance I didn't yet understand."

His gaze strayed out the window, settling somewhere in the trees.

"I think perhaps I was jealous," he murmured thoughtfully. "At any rate, I'm sorry to have said something—especially before you were ready. I'll do anything I can to make it right."

Evie stared at him in astonishment, tears welling in the corners of her eyes. Then all at once, her heart faltered and the color drained from her face.

"Ellanden—"

"I'm serious," he insisted, "anything at all. If you'd like to smooth things over with our parents, I can send for some liquor. If you'd like to spend the night together, I can call in a favor with the guards."

Asher had gone completely rigid.

"*Landi*—"

The fae held up both hands, feeling immensely proud of himself for the entire exchange.

"All I'm trying to say is that of all the people in the world, I'm truly happy the two of you have settled on each other. Such a thing should be celebrated, never hidden away."

He flashed a beatific smile, then turned to leave.

...only to see Dylan Hale standing behind him.

There was a moment when everything paused. Then the fae reached for the plant in a quiet panic, pressing it silently into the king's arms.

Seven hells.

THE FAE VANISHED QUICKER than humanly possible and the three who remained swiftly relocated outside. None of them made a conscious effort to do so, they simply headed towards the courtyard at the same time. Perhaps they needed fresh air. Perhaps they needed witnesses.

As they paused beneath the lilac trees, that tranquil silence felt abruptly mocking. Where were those garish distractions? The terrors that had been following them across the realm.

Evie took a single look at her father, then made a valiant attempt to head things off.

"He was talking about someone else."

...*not my best effort.*

Dylan stared at her for a long moment, then his eyes drifted to the vampire. "...*you?*" he asked with a touch of surprise, a little smile dancing around his lips.

Asher wisely moved not a muscle, but Evie threw a sharp look between them.

"Yes, *him*. Why do you say it like that?"

"Cass and I always joked...I thought if anyone..." His eyes drifted to where Ellanden was spying up above before returning to the vampire. "You were the one I never worried about."

Now it was Asher's turn to look offended, while the princess nodded wisely.

"Because he's the responsible one." She gave him a nudge. "See? I told you."

Dylan stared a moment longer, then clapped his hands briskly. "No matter. It's obviously not allowed, so now that you children are back from the wilderness I'll expect all such nonsense to stop immediately."

Evie tried to arrange her features into something she assumed to be practical. "Father, you can't possibly—"

"*Immediately*, Asher."

The king may not have known it would be the vampire, but he had clearly prepared for such a moment. Step one: verbal threats. Step two: physical intimidation. Step three: ...probably death.

Except we're NOT children! We've fought a basilisk! We've learned to cook!

She turned to Asher with a look of supreme confidence, only to see that he'd turned pale as a sheet. Under the king's piercing eyes he nodded swiftly and backed away.

"...see you at dinner."

Seriously?!

Evie turned back to her father in exasperation, only to find him looking rather smug. The door opened behind him and the vampire slipped out just as Cassiel was coming back in.

"Oh, well done," she snapped before turning expectantly to the fae. "Uncle Cass—did you just see what happened!"

"I certainly did."

He took off his cloak and headed towards them, clapping as he went.

"And I must say, Dylan, you handled that with all the maturity and poise I've come to expect. Nine generations of ghoulish ancestors salute you."

The princess stifled a grin. She hadn't heard much about her father's lineage—stories had been deliberately scarce. But the few things that *had* slipped out weren't pretty.

"Laugh it up," Dylan replied evenly. "Your son is dating a witch."

The fae lifted his shoulders in a shrug.

"I married a shape-shifter. Perhaps such things run in the family." His friend nodded with a meaningful look, and he glanced abruptly towards the overhanging balcony. "...I see your point."

A second later, he was moving straight back the way he'd come.

"Ellanden?" he called as he went. "Take a walk with me."

The fae vanished into the villa, presumably to have a discussion about the wonders of abstinence. Evie stood side by side with her father, watching with a sly smile.

"I'm afraid that ship has sailed," she murmured. "Many, many times."

Dylan chuckled quietly, folding his arms across his chest. "A father can hope..."

Her face stilled and she glanced up at him. "...are you angry about Asher?"

He opened his mouth to answer, then silently shook his head.

Her heart leapt in her chest.

"Do you think that maybe—"

"Everly, I'm going to pretend the concept of you and Asher doesn't exist until the day some beast of darkness finally kills me. Is that understood?"

She slid her hand into his with a secret smile. "Understood."

Chapter 13

As it turned out, the friends didn't have dinner that night. The vampires had already been supplied with blood, and almost as soon as Cassiel had returned to the villa he was called back again by the High Council. This time, the rest of the young monarchs went with him. The friends milled around the villa, feeling once more as if they'd been somehow demoted, then eventually fell asleep.

When Evie awoke the next morning, she was greeted by a familiar smell. "...is something burning?"

An ominous silence echoed in the halls.

Crap.

Without a second thought she leapt out of bed, threw on the nearest dress, and ran barefoot to the kitchen—just in time to find her aunt putting out a small fire.

"Good morning!" the shape-shifter greeted cheerfully. "Eggs?"

The adrenaline faded as Evie flashed her a sleepy smile. "Sounds great."

Still feeling as though she was half-asleep, she wandered blearily to the table to find Cosette and Seth already sitting at it. Judging by the general silence she was guessing her parents were in yet another conclave, and the whereabouts of the rest of her friends were anyone's guess.

"Just try it," Cosette was coaxing, lifting a spoon to the shifter's mouth.

It was one of the first times the two had been openly affectionate, but things had changed ever since the wolf's showdown with the Belarian king. His eyes sparkled as he tried a little bite.

—and jerked back with a start.

"It's *freezing.*"

"It's ice cream," the fae said with a smile, licking the spoon herself. "When we were growing up, there was an entire year that Ellanden refused to eat anything else."

The shifter laughed quietly, but took another spoon for himself. "That doesn't surprise me."

There was a blur of shadow as Asher swept into the room, fastening his cloak with one hand as he reached for his boots with another. "Morning!"

The others said it back, but Evie stared in silence from the table. He'd been suspiciously absent from the villa as well. Since abandoning her in the courtyard, she'd yet to even see him.

"Try this." Seth dug a spoon into the nearest ramekin and extended it without thinking, utterly enchanted with the dessert. "Seriously, Ash, it's the best thing I've ever tasted."

Asher paused behind his chair. "That's butter."

There was a pause.

"And I'm a vampire."

The shifter retracted it with a blush, muttering under his breath. "...why is everything here so difficult?"

"You get out what you put in." Asher breezed away behind him, giving his aunt a quick kiss on the cheek before heading to the door. "I have some errands to run—be back later."

The others responded in unison once again, while Evie stared back in astonishment.

Seriously?! He's not even going to LOOK at me?!

Since she couldn't quite admit to what was happening, she asked something else instead.

"We just got back after a ten-year absence. What errands does he *possibly* have to run?"

"He's a vampire," Cosette said practically. "He's probably going to kill someone."

Seth shuddered involuntarily, while Evie stabbed at her eggs.

"Don't even joke. I'm surprised Leonor didn't try to fit him with a muzzle."

Not that I'd be objecting to that right about now...

There was a sudden noise in the courtyard, and she lifted her head to see Freya and Ellanden standing under the lilacs. There was something very peculiar about their posture and something very serious about their faces, yet every so often they'd burst into a spontaneous bout of laughter.

"What are they doing?" Evie asked curiously.

Cosette glanced out the window before returning to her eggs.

"There's so much raw energy in this place, Landi's been trying to tap into it and shift. He's been working on it all morning. I think he wants to impress his gran."

Evie stared through the glass in surprise.

Although the others hadn't yet been told, it wasn't the first time the fae had dabbled in magic. Just a few days earlier, he'd banished a thunderstorm using nothing but his mind.

Perhaps shape-shifting wasn't that far out of reach.

That being said, he was having a hard time staying focused.

"Just try it," he coaxed.

Freya shook her head, breathless with laughter.

"Come on—try it." His eyes twinkled as he made a supreme effort to clear his face. "I won't do anything, I promise."

Tanya paused by the window, skillet in hand.

"She's getting him to do magic?" she asked in astonishment.

Cosette shook her head. "She's getting him to *resist* magic. It's a little mind-control trick—she used to practice on me all the time. Sneaking inside my head, trying to make me do things."

Evie glanced over with a shiver.

Good thing you learned that lesson. Otherwise we'd still be in a cave.

"Just try it," Ellanden pressed.

"You'll hate it!" Freya laughed. "Cosette usually tried to punch me afterwards."

The people inside turned to the woodland princess.

"That's true," she shrugged.

They turned back to the window.

"You never know...I might surprise you." Ellanden pulled the witch closer, wrapping his long fingers around her wrists. "Or I might not. You might be able to make me do anything your heart desires..." He leaned down with a grin, whispering a wicked secret into her ear.

Whatever it was, the witch made up her mind.

"All right—hold still."

She lifted her fingers to his face, running them lightly across his forehead before slipping them into his hair. A faint shimmer rippled in the air around her before she took a sudden step away.

"Walk to me," she commanded.

The others watched with sudden interest as every hint of expression faded from the prince's face. His eyes lost focus for a moment and his body tensed, as if preparing to take a step.

...but he never did.

"Impressive," Tanya murmured, eyes dancing with pride.

"That's really good!" Freya echoed outside, skipping back to him. "It took Cosette ages to hold out like that. I can still get her sometimes, if she's not paying attention."

The woodland princess flushed. "...that's a lie."

"Try it again," Ellanden said eagerly, thrilled to have discovered a new skill. "Something else this time. Something harder."

The witch considered a moment before stepping up to him with a smile.

"Kiss me."

Another wave of enchantment washed over the fae, but this time his lips twitched in a secret smile. He stood completely motionless a split second before picking her up right off her feet.

"If you insist..."

The others turned swiftly back to the table as the two came together in a passionate embrace. Only Tanya remained, staring a moment longer before returning to the kitchen.

"I'm sure Gran will be thrilled," Evie teased.

Cosette grinned into her plate.

"What's she like?" Seth asked curiously.

"*Well...*" Evie began importantly, ticking things off her fingers, "she's about nine thousand years old, she wears mostly deceased reptiles, and..." She trailed off suddenly, looking at him with delight. "...and you're a very handsome man, Seth."

He glanced up in surprise. "Uh...thank you?"

Those dark eyes flickered to his girlfriend, but Cosette was grinning as well.

"You really are," she murmured. "I never thought of it like that."

"We could style him up a little," Evie suggested. "Or maybe style him down. Take off some of those cumbersome clothes."

Seth stared between them in bewilderment. "What are you talking about?"

Tanya swooped in from the kitchen, dumping another mountain of eggs onto their plates.

"Gran's going to *love* you."

EVIE PROLONGED BREAKFAST as much as she could, then decided to go find her wayward boyfriend herself. Because he was still her boyfriend. Because her father didn't get to decide that.

She was just heading out the door as her mother came back in.

"Oh!" she stepped back in surprise. "Are you done already?"

Katerina froze in the doorway, then collected herself quickly.

"No, I was just coming to get Tanya. She's still the queen of this land," she added in a low undertone, "even if some people have forgotten."

Evie tilted her head curiously. "What?"

Her mother shook her head. "Is she here?"

"Yeah, she's setting fires in the kitchen." Evie reached behind her to a box that had been left beside the door. "Did you drop something?"

Katerina frowned in confusion. "No, someone must have sent it up."

She took it from her daughter and cracked it open, suddenly going still. A strange expression swept over her. One that made Evie feel relieved to see her grandmother coming up the hall.

"What is that?" Adelaide asked curiously, peering inside.

The lid fell back to reveal a crown. The same crown for which Katerina and her friends had set off on a journey of their own, waging wars and uniting kingdoms. The same crown that had granted them immortality for as long as she'd worn it, courtesy of the glowing ruby stone.

...left in a box by the door.

Evie stared at the ruby with fresh eyes, wondering if it was somehow aware they were on a mission to destroy its twin. But Katerina was looking at her mother, realizing it was the first time in decades that she'd seen her beloved stone.

"I broke my promise," she said lightly. "I told you I'd never take it off."

The words were casual, but there was a tightness in them all the same. Adelaide glanced up in surprise before running a gentle hand along her daughter's hair.

"You didn't break anything," she murmured. "Nothing that can't be fixed."

A silent look passed between them, then Katerina made an effort to save face.

"For what it's worth, I liked it better as a necklace."

Adelaide lifted it with a smile, placing it atop her daughter's head. "It looks better in a crown."

EVIE WANDERED AROUND the pavilion for a while, making polite small talk with strangers and searching for her missing boyfriend before heading back to the villa. She'd been in a strange mood since that morning, and couldn't stop picturing her mother in the crown.

Why did they just leave it there? she wondered as she trudged back into the house. *Why was there no messenger or ceremony? We don't even know who brought it back...*

She walked into her room, only to be greeted by a most peculiar sight.

A princess with fiery red hair sitting on her bed.

What the—

The girl shrieked as Evie picked up a blade, waving it between them.

"Don't—it's just me!"

What?!

"I'M me!" she exclaimed. "What the hell are you—"

"It's Ellanden!"

WHAT?!

"Close the door!" The girl furiously stalked past her, slamming it shut before yanking the dagger right out of her hands. "Why is *that* your instinct? You see yourself and grab a blade?"

The princess froze, then took a step closer.

"No...you're not the one who gets to ask questions right now." She tilted her head in amazement, watching as the girl unconsciously did the same. "Now what on earth—"

"I was trying to shape-shift and I got stuck," the fae said miserably, sinking in despair onto the bed. "You're supposed to think of someone and—"

"And you thought of me?" the princess interrupted, surprisingly touched.

"I wasn't thinking I wanted to BE you! Help me change back!"

There was a knock at the door.

"Who is it?" both Evies called at the same time.

"It's Asher."

"Seven hells, this isn't happening." Ellanden closed his eyes in horror, but by the time he opened them the real princess was already gone. "Everly! Where did you—"

The door pushed open and the vampire stepped inside. "Hey...can I come in?"

Ellanden froze, then shook his head. "It's not really a good time. Why don't you come back later?"

Asher flinched with quiet sigh. "You're right to be angry. I didn't mean to take off on you like that. There were just some things that I needed to—"

"I'm not angry," Ellanden interrupted quickly, glancing around the room. "Not angry at all, I promise. Just, uh...let's do this at a different—"

"Evie." The vampire was in front of him a second later, staring down with remorse. "I really *am* sorry. Your father threw me a little, and I...I needed to figure some things out."

The real princess watched with wide eyes from the closet, wondering what those things were. Ellanden fidgeted uncomfortably, highly disconcerted by the feeling of wearing a dress.

"Okay, well...don't worry about it. It's fine."

Asher's eyebrows lifted slowly. "It's fine?"

It's not fine.

"It's not *fine*," Ellanden amended quickly, then flashed a tight smile. "But we're good." He fidgeted again, chafing against the fabric swishing around his legs. "You can...you can go now."

Asher reached down with a smile, tilting up his chin. "What's going on? You're acting strange."

The fae jerked back like his hands were on fire.

"Strange?" he asked a little breathlessly. "No, just...busy. *Very* busy. I'd like you to leave."

He backed away discreetly, glancing out the window as if Evie might have simply leapt outside, then jumped with the vampire caught him lightly by the elbow.

"I'm serious—talk to me. What's wrong?"

Ellanden straightened in frustration, unaccustomed to seeing him from such a low height. "Are you always this clingy?"

Asher froze in surprise, then let out a burst of laughter. "Clingy?"

"I mean—" The fae caught himself quickly, sensing that a better explanation would be required. "The thing is, I just...I have all these...feelings."

Asher's eyebrows lifted delicately, while Evie snorted into her sleeve.

"Okay..."

He sat down on the edge of the bed, only for the fae to grab him reflexively by the cloak and pull him back up again. "No, that's not...don't do that."

Asher glanced incredulously at the mattress. "Do what?"

"*All these feelings*," the fae repeated, getting them back on track. "Well, they often get on top of me, and a lot's been going on these last few days, and I need some time to think."

Asher stared a moment, then nodded.

"Yeah, of course." He took a step towards the door, then paused. "But you and me...we're good? I'm not one of those things you need to think about?"

Ellanden nodded quickly, fingers drumming on the side of his legs. "We're good."

The vampire stared a moment longer, examining him with a frown. But when he came up with nothing he nodded with a faint smile, giving that fiery hair a tug.

"Ash—" Ellanden took a step back, gently pulling free.

Asher laughed again. "What is wrong with you today?"

The fae actually considered it for a moment. "I'd have to say this isn't too far off from normal."

Bugger.

"All right, well you just think then. I'll see you at dinner."

"Great. 'Bye."

The fae had already turned around, so he didn't see the vampire lean down with an automatic kiss. By the time he did, it was all he could do to turn his face so it landed on his cheek.

"That's—" He caught himself again, pulling back with a tight smile. "Uh...thanks." As if it wasn't bad enough, he patted the vampire awkwardly on top of the head. "'Bye, Asher."

It was all Evie could do to keep from laughing. It was all Asher could do to keep from having his girlfriend declared officially insane. He swept into the hall with a quiet laugh, shutting the door behind him. Ellanden stared at it bracingly before turning around with a scathing glare.

"Get out here...*now*."

She let out a forbidden giggle, and he dragged her out by the hair.

"Oh, I'm sorry—is this funny?" he demanded. "You been harboring secret fantasies all these years? Really want to see me and your boyfriend make out?"

"It would be an interesting way to end the day..."

"I'm going to *strangle* you. Help me change back."

"All right...did you have a plan for that?"

He picked up a heavy paperweight and thrust it into her hands. "Here."

She blinked down at it, eyes travelling slowly back to her own face. "You want me to bludgeon you with this?"

The fae nodded swiftly, glancing at the door. "Yes, hurry."

"Landi—"

"Just hard enough to knock me out. I can't stay shifted when I'm knocked out, right?" He glanced again at the door, worried the vampire might return. "Hurry, Everly. Before someone else comes in."

With a martyred sigh she lifted the paperweight, only to lower it again. "I can't do it. I can't hit myself."

He put it back in her hand. "You've never had *any* trouble hitting me before."

"I'm going to need therapy!"

It was remarkable how, despite wearing someone else's face, the fae still managed to convey such a range of emotion. He pulled in a quick breath, searching for patience while imagining what it might be like to bludgeon her instead.

"Everly, for such a *great many things*, this won't even make the list. Now DO it!"

The paperweight flew between them.

"...OW!"

"You were supposed to black out!"

"You were supposed to *make* me black out!"

There was a split second pause then they grabbed for the weight at the same time, trying to wrestle it away from each other.

"Give it back!" Evie cried, "I'm going to try again!"

Several hundred times.

"Seven hells, princess! How are you this weak??" Ellanden demanded, horrified at his newfound limitations, as he was unable to pull it away.

She slapped him in the face.

"Yes, just like that. But much harder!"

"Oh, I'm going to *kill* you..."

A throat cleared softly and the two of them turned to see Asher watching by the door. He stared at them for a moment, impossible to read, then tilted his head with a little smile.

"Yeah...you've got some feelings to sort out."

THE TWO PRINCESSES were sitting on the bed. Asher was sitting between them.

It hadn't taken long to recount the story, strange as it was, but once it was finished neither one of them could transition into the next thing. It wasn't until Evie caught sight of their reflection in the mirror that she pushed abruptly to her feet and disappeared once more into the closet.

"I'll be right back..."

The boys nodded in silence. After a few seconds, Asher gave the fae a sideways glance.

"So that was you that I almost—"

"Yep."

"And it couldn't have been—"

"Nope."

"Probably best if we never—"

"Yep."

They sat a moment longer, then Asher shot him a look.

"I'm *not* clingy."

Evie joined them a second later with a bright scarf, thinking herself quite clever.

"There," she declared, wrapping it around her neck. "Now you can tell us apart."

"No need," Asher said with a faint grin. "I already can."

"You couldn't before," Ellanden muttered, then lifted a hand to the blood on his face. "Wait—this? Because of *this*?!"

The vampire shrugged unapologetically, while Evie turned with sudden curiosity.

"What does mine smell like—"

"NOT THE TIME!"

For the next few minutes Evie and Asher went back and forth, spouting different theories as to how best to help him while Ellanden sat with increasing despondence on the bed. They covered everything, from sleeping draughts to meditation. It might have carried on even longer if the princess hadn't glanced over to see him feeling discreetly at the sides of his dress.

"What are you doing?" she asked suddenly.

He jumped guiltily, hands flying back to his lap. "Nothing."

Asher took a step forward.

"What *are* you doing?" he repeated sharply.

The fae froze a moment, then answered in a voice much quieter than his own.

"...how does one breathe in a corset?"

The vampire quickly looked away, while Evie's hands flew up to her hair.

"We have GOT to fix this. NOW!"

"WHAT HAPPENED TO YOUR face?"

The three friends glanced up at the same time, seated at a long dining table with the rest of their family. Unlike most nights, they'd decided to dine with the rest of the court in the great hall.

Ellanden stared at his girlfriend, then looked quickly down at his plate.

"Must have run into a door..."

They had decided to go with the bludgeoning idea after all. The instant Evie mentioned it, the vampire seemed to think it was a marvelous idea and picked up the paperweight at once.

The result was a rather massive concussion that seemed unlikely to ever fully heal.

But it had worked. The fae was himself.

"Never again," he muttered under his breath.

The princess tried very hard to keep a straight face, while Asher clapped him on the shoulder with a wicked grin. "What was that, pumpkin?"

The fae jerked away with a glare. "...*never* again."

Dylan glanced over from a couple of places down.

"What are they talking about?" he asked curiously.

"Children's troubles," Cassiel replied without much thought. "One of them got trapped in another's shape."

The king nodded to himself, then looked up with sudden curiosity. "Have you and Tanya ever...?"

The fae gave him a look that silenced the conversation forever. "...twice."

Dylan raised his eyebrows slowly.

"I don't want to talk about it."

Meanwhile, the shifter was having a fine time on the other side of the table—regaling his girlfriend with story after story in an effort to make her laugh. The others were soon drawn in as well, contributing tales of their own. Wine was flowing, the conversation was brightening, and things were just starting to pick up speed, when Ellanden crushed a goblet with his bare hand.

The friends looked over in surprise as wine and glass spilled all over the table. They stared a moment, then lifted their eyes to the fae—who glanced away with a flush.

"Just checking..."

Asher pursed his lips, glancing down at the table. "You didn't want to empty it first?"

The princess pushed graciously to her feet. "I'll get you a new one."

With a little smile she wound through the dining hall, shooting covert glances all the while at the fae. It was a completely different atmosphere than at the Belarian palace. One that was equally lighthearted while being infinitely more composed. At least, it was *usually* lighthearted.

While the hall rang out with laughter and music, she couldn't help but notice the slight layer of tension. That laughter was stilted. That conversation had an edge.

Ouch!

A fae knocked into her as he walked past.

He had jet black hair and eyes as green as leaves. Unlike most of the others in the hall, he looked about her age. But he was glaring with a hundred years' worth of rage.

"*Tegalin.*"

There was a sudden scraping as Ellanden pushed up from his chair. "Jarieze!"

A hush of silence fell over the hall.

The fae turned that steely glare towards the prince before sinking into a stiff bow and stalking out of the room. The others looked up in surprise, but made no effort to stop him.

What the hell just happened?

With a pointed glanced from the high table, the music started back up. The conversation started back up a second later. Evie forgot the goblet and headed straight back to her chair.

"Are you okay?" Asher asked in a quiet voice, fighting the urge to take off after the fae who'd slighted her. Judging by some of the other looks at the table, he wasn't the only one.

She shook her head quickly, trying to calm things down.

"I'm fine. It was my mistake," she added quickly. "I knocked into him."

Why did I just say that?

The others watched her for a moment, as if waiting for signs of distress before returning to their meal. Her father was holding a knife. Cassiel was staring quietly at the door.

She watched them a moment before shooting a quick glance at the prince.

"What does *tegalin* mean?"

Ellanden gritted his teeth. She could tell he didn't want to tell her. He wanted to take off after the male and beat him to a pulp. He took a deep breath instead, lowering his eyes to the table.

"It means traitor."

Chapter 14

"We were kidnapped!"

"I know."

"*Kidnapped*!" the princess repeated. "For ten years! With some monster sucking the life out of us! It's not like we've been lounging!"

"I know."

"Not to mention the only reason we left in the first place was to save the realm from total annihilation, even knowing at least one of us was going to die!"

There was a pause.

"I know."

"And the look on that guy's face—"

Ellanden caught her suddenly by the shoulders, spinning her around to face the cliff. There was an involuntary pause, as if some higher power had stolen her very breath. Then—

"Okay, you're right...I feel better."

The friends had escaped the dining hall as quickly as possible then left the city altogether, following the fae as he led them higher onto the peaks. He'd assured her the climb would be worth it. He'd assured her it would take her mind off what had happened.

He hadn't been wrong.

It's overwhelming.

Like everything else in the Ivory City, the beauty was almost too much to bear. The princess' eyes teared up immediately as her gaze rose above the waterfalls into an infinity of stars.

"My father used to bring me up here," Ellanden said quietly, lifting his eyes beside her. "He'd sneak me out when the rest of the city was sleeping. Taught me all the constellations by name."

The others gazed up alongside him, feeling uncharacteristically small.

"What's that one?" Freya asked, pointing towards a particularly bright design.

Ellanden smiled, following her gaze. "Those are the lovers. Not much is known about them. When my people die, they're said to ascend into a kind of heaven. All of us summoned back to the stars."

Asher glanced at him curiously. "To live as angels?"

The fae shook his head with a smile. "To live as servants. To serve at our creator's feet."

Freya peered up beside him. "...forever?"

He wrapped an arm around her shoulders. "Not forever. Until some version of this place is made new and we can walk the earth once more." His eyes drifted back to the constellation. "Only the most marked of us receive such honor."

Evie followed his gaze, wondering who they were.

The friends were quiet for a while, then Seth glanced over—studying the fae's expression with a wicked smile. "...and what does your grandmother think about all that?"

The others laughed quietly, still staring at the sky.

"My gran once told me I'd be reincarnated as a newt," Ellanden replied with a grin. "I try not to pester her with existential questions."

That's a good call.

They stood there a while longer, lost in the heavens.

"What really happened in the dining hall?" Cosette asked softly. "Why would that man have done such a thing? Why would no one have punished him? Not even the council..."

A kind of chill fell over them, cutting through the balmy breeze. They shivered beneath it, realizing it wasn't new. Realizing it had been there the whole time.

"I'm not sure," Asher replied quietly, "but it was the same way in the city. There is a tension to this place that didn't used to be here. An anger...though I'm not sure it's directed at any person."

He caught the witch's pointed glance, and rolled his eyes.

"No, Freya—not even at me. I may have committed the unspeakable crime of being born a vampire, but most of these people have known me since I was a child. And it was not me who drew their ire in the dining hall, but a princess they love much better than myself."

Evie shivered again, remembering the look in the fae's eyes.

Traitor.

Did they really think such a thing? After everything that had happened?

A part of her was enraged. Another part couldn't help asking the obvious question.

...how could they not?

"Come on," Cosette said quietly. "We should get back to the villa. Our parents will start to wonder where we've gone."

The friends nodded silently and started trekking back down the mountain trail, casting a final look at the heavens before they vanished into the trees. The princess headed automatically after them, but paused when Asher caught her lightly by the wrist.

"Could you stay a moment?"

She turned in surprise, a surprise that tripled when she saw his expression. "Of course. What's wrong?"

Never had she seen the vampire so nervous, not even when they were standing in front of the vampire queen. His pale skin seemed almost to glow in the moonlight and his eyes were full of stars. His gaze rested on her carefully, unable to hide that underlying fear.

"So I realize you probably heard my apology this afternoon, but I said it by mistake to Ellanden and never got to say the same words to you." He stared a second longer, then reached into his pocket and pulled out a string of dazzling gems. "I got this for you today in the city—that's where I went after breakfast. I wanted to tell you…but I also wanted it to be a surprise."

It certainly was.

Evie stared in amazement as he lifted shimmering jewels, as if asking for permission before slipping it gently around her neck.

Her fingers came up immediately to touch it, tracing the edges of the stones.

"Do you like it?" he asked softly. "I remember you seeing a similar thing at the carnival the night before we left. I wanted to buy it for you then, but hadn't brought any coin."

She warmed with a smile, remembering the same thing.

"That's right…Asher, I *love* it. Thank you."

Their eyes met shyly, then he leaned down with a gentle kiss.

"I'm sorry your father found out like that," he murmured, "and I'm sorry that I took off the way I did. To be honest, it seemed like the only way to avoid getting stabbed." He paused with a little smile, but it faded as he stared into her eyes. "But Evie, you have to know that nothing like that will ever matter. At least, not to me. Ellanden was right—what he said to us. I'm in love with you. In a way I didn't think possible. In a way I didn't know I needed. In a way I could never be without."

She stared up in breathless silence as his hands cupped her face.

"When my father walked in on us that day, when he said that he didn't see…he wasn't talking about the bond. I'll tell him about that later. He was talking about the love."

He glanced down suddenly, almost afraid to meet her eyes.

"Such a thing changes a vampire…in a tangible way. Opening your heart to another person, surrendering it so completely…" He trailed into silence, then his eyes flickered up to the stars. "I would imagine it's a bit like that constellation. It's too great a thing to be confined to this place."

She stared a moment longer, then kissed him without thinking—throwing herself into him with the same reckless abandon as the two came together under the stars.

A tear slipped down her cheek as she pressed a hand to his chest.

"That's why I can feel this?" she whispered. "I always tried before, but I never could."

His eyes softened with a tender smile.

"Neither could I."

THE PRINCESS STARED *across the ballroom, feeling as though she'd been there before. The setting was unfamiliar, but the people were the same. All those eternal eyes that'd watched her in the forests of Taviel. All those Belarian children who'd danced before her in the streets. Her eyes blurred as they danced past in a sea of faces, twirling to life in front of her before vanishing. The entire room was moving, but two faces stood still in the crowd.*

A man she'd known forever. Another that she'd recently come to love.

Both of them took a step towards her... but there could be only one.

Evie awoke with a gasp, the string of diamonds biting into her neck. She lifted a hand to loosen it, trying to slow her pounding heartbeat as the familiar chorus of voices drifted up the hall.

"—tried it the first time, but it's hard to slip such a thing past the guards—"

She dropped her feet to the floor, feeling strangely light-headed as she dressed quickly and headed outside to join them. Sure enough, her friends were in the kitchen. Their parents were gone.

"Where is everyone?" she asked, fighting back a rising sense of dread.

At some point in the night, it had taken hold of her. Her fingers were trembling with it now.

"They went back to the citadel," Cosette answered, "called to another meeting."

Ellanden shot a glance towards the ivory towers.

"At this rate, we should have continued on to the Dunes without them," he murmured, joking only a little. "Let them worry about uniting the kingdoms themselves—"

"*No.*"

The rest of the room went silent as the friends looked up in surprise. The princess was standing before them, but they didn't quite recognize her expression. A strange kind of resolve had come over her, burning like fire in her eyes.

"Get dressed," she said quietly. "We're going to this meeting."

THE STREETS OF TAVIEL were abandoned and quiet, but as they neared the gleaming citadel a swarm of angry voices drifted out to greet them before they'd even reached the door.

They came to a collective pause, then quietly pushed open the door.

Seven hells...

Evie understood now why their parents had looked so worn each time they returned from the citadel. It was the same expression they'd worn in Belaria; although, then, it had been easier to hide. They stood now in the center of the dais, trying desperately to maintain order, but it was like watching a group of people trying to hold back the tide.

It was chaos. Complete and utter chaos.

"—asking us to do such a thing, but it has been *years* since we fought alongside the High Kingdom," a fae was shouting. "Where were the wolves of Belaria when the outpost at Cadarest was overrun by the Carpathians? Where were your queen's knights when the giants attacked?"

His voice was lost in a sea of so many others, the princess couldn't possibly keep track. The council of the fae was trying to keep order, but to her astonishment it looked as though many of them didn't disagree. It was the same thing she'd seen hints of in Belaria. The same reason their parents had seen no reason to stop in the High Kingdom. The reason the Kreo had yet to arrive.

The realm has been broken...no hint of alliance has survived.

"We will fight alongside you, my lord." A fae in gleaming armor pushed slowly to his feet, bowing his head to Cassiel as a group of others rose behind him. "We will fight alongside you until the stars vanish from the sky. But we have no remaining ties to those who stand beside you. If you wish to lead the fae into battle against this new darkness, we answer only to you—"

"Then you will all perish!" Dylan shouted, not for the first time. "How is it possible I've failed to make myself clear? This fight is bigger than any one group of people can withstand. Unless the kingdoms unite—"

"An eloquent point, Your Majesty," another warrior interrupted. "One that would have carried a great deal more weight had you not *left* the kingdoms to carry the weight of such darkness alone. You expect to wave a hand and fix all that was broken? *Lives* have been lost. This is not a wound that can so easily be mended—"

Back and forth they went, one spiraling after another. For a split second the princess felt as though she was back in that ballroom, trying to find balance as a blur of people danced by.

A feeling of intense cold swept over her, as if she'd suddenly stepped out of the sun. Every instinct rose up in rebellion, but she turned with a strange calm to the boy at her side.

"Whatever happens, you'll be right there beside me." She quoted the same words he'd said in Belaria, staring up into the vampire's eyes. "You promise?"

Asher's lips parted uncertainly before he finished the line.

"Always."

Forgive me.

"People of the realm—allow me to speak!"

In hindsight, she'd never know how they heard her. A lone voice amidst a chorus of others, but every person in the citadel turned to her at the same time.

"What in the seven hells are you doing?" Ellanden whispered behind her.

The rest of them were staring with the same astonishment. Just over their heads, she saw the same expression reflected by their parents—a breathless kind of panic flickering in their eyes.

"I understand that you're angry," she said in a shaky voice, trying not to tremble as a city of faces stared back at her. "You feel betrayed and abandoned. Blood has been spilled, lives have been lost, and you are left searching for some kind of relief. Please understand that such a thing was never our intent. My friends and I set out only to fulfill a prophecy, to drive back the very darkness of which you speak. But it seems the fates had something else in mind."

She paused a second before forcing herself forward.

"My father was right in what he said. This is not the kind of fight that any one kingdom can survive on its own. We must unite or we will be destroyed—and that darkness will take hold once and for all. In the past, such alliances were assured by marriage."

Katerina's face went pale as Dylan pushed halfway to his feet.

"Everly—"

She lifted a hand to silence him, steeling herself with a breath.

Their parents had stood in front of them long enough. Sheltering, protecting. Angling themselves between their children and all those terrible truths they'd never want them to see.

But they were children no longer. It was time to grow up.

She turned instead to the pair of men in front of her. Closer than brothers, standing side by side. The fae was frozen in astonishment as the vampire lit up with a preemptive smile.

"Ellanden...will you marry me?"

THE END

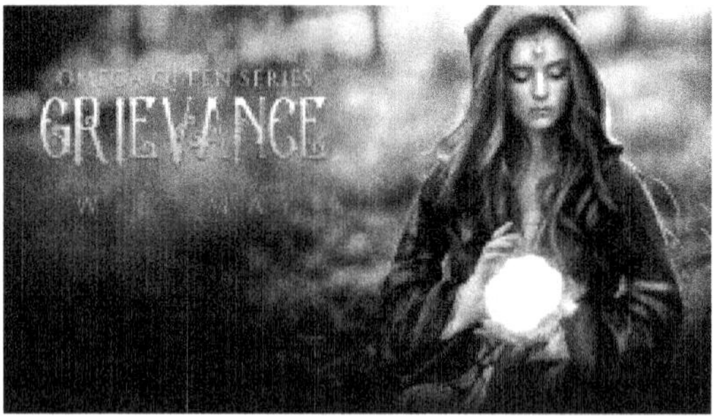
GRIEVANCE

Grievance Blurb

The Queen's Alpha Series

Eternal
Everlasting
Unceasing
Evermore
Forever
Boundless
Prophecy
Protected
Foretelling
Revelation
Betrayal
Resolved

The Omega Queen Series

Discipline
Bravery
Courage
Conquer
Strength
Validation
Approval
Blessing
Balance
Grievance
Enchanted
Gratified

Find W.J. May

Website:
http://www.wjmaybooks.com
Facebook:
https://www.facebook.com/pages/Author-WJ-May-FAN-PAGE/141170442608149
Newsletter:
SIGN UP FOR W.J. May's Newsletter to find out about new releases, updates, cover reveals and even freebies!
http://eepurl.com/97aYf

More books by W.J. May

The Chronicles of Kerrigan

Book I - *Rae of Hope* is FREE!
Book Trailer:
http://www.youtube.com/watch?v=gILAwXxx8MU
Book II - *Dark Nebula*
Book Trailer:
http://www.youtube.com/watch?v=Ca24STi_bFM
Book III - *House of Cards*
Book IV - *Royal Tea*
Book V - *Under Fire*
Book VI - *End in Sight*
Book VII – *Hidden Darkness*
Book VIII – *Twisted Together*
Book IX – *Mark of Fate*
Book X – *Strength & Power*
Book XI – *Last One Standing*
BOOK XII – *Rae of Light*

PREQUEL –
Christmas Before the Magic

BALANCE

Question the Darkness
Into the Darkness
Fight the Darkness
Alone the Darkness
Lost the Darkness

SEQUEL –
    Matter of Time
    Time Piece
    Second Chance
    Glitch in Time
    Our Time
    Precious Time

Hidden Secrets Saga:
Download Seventh Mark part 1 For FREE
Book Trailer:
http://www.youtube.com/watch?v=Y-_vVYC1gvo

Like most teenagers, Rouge is trying to figure out who she is and what she wants to be. With little knowledge about her past, she has questions but has never tried to find the answers. Everything changes when she befriends a strangely intoxicating family. Siblings Grace and Michael, appear to have secrets which seem connected to Rouge. Her hunch is confirmed when a horrible incident occurs at an outdoor party. Rouge may be the only one who can find the answer.

An ancient journal, a Sioghra necklace and a special mark force life-altering decisions for a girl who grew up unprepared to fight for her life or others.

All secrets have a cost and Rouge's determination to find the truth can only lead to trouble...or something even more sinister.

RADIUM HALOS - THE SENSELESS SERIES
Book 1 is FREE

Everyone needs to be a hero at one point in their life.

The small town of Elliot Lake will never be the same again.

Caught in a sudden thunderstorm, Zoe, a high school senior from Elliot Lake, and five of her friends take shelter in an abandoned uranium mine. Over the next few days, Zoe's hearing sharpens drastically, beyond what any normal human being can detect. She tells her friends, only to learn that four others have an increased sense as well. Only Kieran, the new boy from Scotland, isn't affected.

Fashioning themselves into superheroes, the group tries to stop the strange occurrences happening in their little town. Muggings, break-ins, disappearances, and murder begin to hit too close to home. It leads the team to think someone knows about their secret - someone who wants them all dead.

An incredulous group of heroes. A traitor in the midst. Some dreams are written in blood.

Courage Runs Red
The Blood Red Series
Book 1 is FREE

WHAT IF COURAGE WAS your only option?

When Kallie lands a college interview with the city's new hot-shot police officer, she has no idea everything in her life is about to change. The detective is young, handsome and seems to have an unnatural ability to stop the increasing local crime rate. Detective Liam's particular interest in Kallie sends her heart and head stumbling over each other.

When a raging blood feud between vampires spills into her home, Kallie gets caught in the middle. Torn between love and family loyalty she must find the courage to fight what she fears the most and possibly risk everything, even if it means dying for those she loves.

Daughter of Darkness - Victoria
Only Death Could Stop Her Now
The Daughters of Darkness is a series of female heroines who may or may not know each other, but all have the same father, Vlad Montour. Victoria is a Hunter Vampire

HUNTRESS SERIES
USA TODAY BESTSELLING AUTHOR
W.J. MAY
LOOK BACK
MASTER
PERMISSION

PROPHECY SERIES
USA TODAY BESTSELLING AUTHOR
• W.J. MAY •
PROPHECY
PROPHECY
PROPHECY

The Chronicles of
KERRIGAN
W.J. May
RAE OF HOPE
DARK NEBULA
HOUSE OF CARDS
ROYAL TEA
UNDER FIRE
END IN SIGHT

THE HIDDEN
SECRETS SAGA
W.J. MAY

Don't miss out!

Visit the website below and you can sign up to receive emails whenever W.J. May publishes a new book. There's no charge and no obligation.

https://books2read.com/r/B-A-SSF-NQHLB

BOOKS 2 READ

Connecting independent readers to independent writers.

Did you love *Balance*? Then you should read *Victoria*[1] by W.J. May!

Victoria

Only Death Could Stop Her Now

The Daughters of Darkness is a series of female heroines who may or may not know each other, but all have the same father, Vlad Montour.

Victoria is a Hunter Vampire, one of the last of her kind. She's the best of the best.

When she finds out one of her marks is actually her sister she lets her go, only to end up on the wrong side of the council.

Forced to prove herself she hunts her next mark, a werewolf. Injured and hungry, she is forced to do what she must to survive. Her ac-

---

1. https://books2read.com/u/bzNLZb

2. https://books2read.com/u/bzNLZb

tions upset the ancient council and she finds herself now being the one thing she has always despised -- the Hunted.

This is Tori's story by W.J. May. This is book 1 of a series, all your questions will not be answered in the first book.

This is an adult book series and does contain scenes for readers that are 16+

4 authors will each take a different daughter born from the Prince of Darkness, Vlad Montour. (Also known as Vlad the Impaler, an evil villain from history)

Blair – Chrissy Peebles

Jezebel – Kristen Middleton

Victoria – W.J. May

Lotus – C.J. Pinard

Victoria's Journey:

Victoria

Huntress

Coveted

Twisted

Read more at www.wjmaybooks.com.

Also by W.J. May

Bit-Lit Series
Lost Vampire
Cost of Blood
Price of Death

Blood Red Series
Courage Runs Red
The Night Watch
Marked by Courage
Forever Night
The Other Side of Fear
Blood Red Box Set Books #1-5

Daughters of Darkness: Victoria's Journey
Victoria
Huntress
Coveted (A Vampire & Paranormal Romance)
Twisted
Daughter of Darkness - Victoria - Box Set

Great Temptation Series
The Devil's Footsteps
Heaven's Command
Mortals Surrender

Hidden Secrets Saga
Seventh Mark - Part 1
Seventh Mark - Part 2
Marked By Destiny
Compelled
Fate's Intervention
Chosen Three
The Hidden Secrets Saga: The Complete Series

Kerrigan Chronicles
Stopping Time
A Passage of Time
Ticking Clock
Secrets in Time
Time in the City
Ultimate Future

Mending Magic Series
Lost Souls
Illusion of Power
Challenging the Dark

Castle of Power
Limits of Magic
Protectors of Light

Omega Queen Series
Discipline
Bravery
Courage
Conquer
Strength
Validation
Approval
Blessing
Balance
Omega Queen - Box Set Books #1-3

Paranormal Huntress Series
Never Look Back
Coven Master
Alpha's Permission
Blood Bonding
Oracle of Nightmares
Shadows in the Night
Paranormal Huntress BOX SET

Prophecy Series
Only the Beginning
White Winter

Secrets of Destiny

Revamped Series
Hidden
Banished
Converted

Royal Factions
The Price For Peace
The Cost for Surviving
The Punishment For Deception
Faking Perfection
The Most Cherished
The Strength to Endure

The Chronicles of Kerrigan
Rae of Hope
Dark Nebula
House of Cards
Royal Tea
Under Fire
End in Sight
Hidden Darkness
Twisted Together
Mark of Fate
Strength & Power
Last One Standing
Rae of Light

The Chronicles of Kerrigan Box Set Books # 1 - 6

The Chronicles of Kerrigan: Gabriel
Living in the Past
Present For Today
Staring at the Future

The Chronicles of Kerrigan Prequel
Christmas Before the Magic
Question the Darkness
Into the Darkness
Fight the Darkness
Alone in the Darkness
Lost in Darkness
The Chronicles of Kerrigan Prequel Series Books #1-3

The Chronicles of Kerrigan Sequel
A Matter of Time
Time Piece
Second Chance
Glitch in Time
Our Time
Precious Time

The Hidden Secrets Saga
Seventh Mark (part 1 & 2)

The Kerrigan Kids
School of Potential
Myths & Magic
Kith & Kin
Playing With Power
Line of Ancestry
Descent of Hope
Illusion of Shadows
Frozen by the Future
Guilt Of My Past
Demise of Magic
The Kerrigan Kids Box Set Books #1-3

The Queen's Alpha Series
Eternal
Everlasting
Unceasing
Evermore
Forever
Boundless
Prophecy
Protected
Foretelling
Revelation
Betrayal
Resolved
The Queen's Alpha Box Set

The Senseless Series
Radium Halos - Part 1
Radium Halos - Part 2
Nonsense
Perception
The Senseless - Box Set Books #1-4

Standalone
Shadow of Doubt (Part 1 & 2)
Five Shades of Fantasy
Zwarte Nevel
Shadow of Doubt - Part 1
Shadow of Doubt - Part 2
Four and a Half Shades of Fantasy
Dream Fighter
What Creeps in the Night
Forest of the Forbidden
Arcane Forest: A Fantasy Anthology
The First Fantasy Box Set

Watch for more at www.wjmaybooks.com.

About the Author

About W.J. May

Welcome to USA TODAY BESTSELLING author W.J. May's Page! SIGN UP for W.J. May's Newsletter to find out about new releases, updates, cover reveals and even freebies! http://eepurl.com/97aYf

Website: http://www.wjmaybooks.com

Facebook: http://www.facebook.com/pages/Author-WJ-May-FAN-PAGE/141170442608149?ref=hl *Please feel free to connect with me and share your comments. I love connecting with my readers.*

W.J. May grew up in the fruit belt of Ontario. Crazy-happy childhood, she always has had a vivid imagination and loads of energy. After her father passed away in 2008, from a six-year battle with cancer (which she still believes he won the fight against), she began to write again. A passion she'd loved for years, but realized life was too short to keep putting it off. She is a writer of Young Adult, Fantasy Fiction and where ever else her little muses take her.

Read more at www.wjmaybooks.com.

Printed in Great Britain
by Amazon